"Randall, that's not possible."

"Sure it is, Lacy."

"It's not. You just can't *do* that!"

"Why?"

"Because."

"Try again."

"No. I don't have your balance. Besides, bathtubs weren't designed for this."

"I can't stand rejection."

"I'm not rejecting you. Oh!"

"Hmmm. Now aren't you glad you tried again?"

Dear Reader:

Spring is here! And we've got six new SECOND CHANCE AT LOVE romances to add to your pleasure in the new season. So sit back, put your feet up, and enjoy . . .

You've also got a lot to look forward to in the months ahead—delightful romances from exciting new writers, as well as fabulous stories from your tried-and-true favorites. You know you can rely on SECOND CHANCE AT LOVE to provide the kind of satisfying romantic entertainment you expect.

We continue to receive and enjoy your letters—so please keep them coming! Remember: Your thoughts and feelings about SECOND CHANCE AT LOVE books are what enable us to publish the kind of romances you not only enjoy reading once, but also keep in a special place and read again and again.

Warm wishes for a beautiful spring,

Ellen Edwards

Ellen Edwards
SECOND CHANCE AT LOVE
The Berkley Publishing Group
200 Madison Avenue
New York, N.Y. 10016

Second Chance at Love®

MOONLIGHT RHAPSODY

KAY ROBBINS

**SECOND CHANCE AT LOVE
BOOK**

Other Second Chance at Love books by
Kay Robbins

RETURN ENGAGEMENT   #73
TAKEN BY STORM   #110
ELUSIVE DAWN   #130
KISSED BY MAGIC   #155

To my parents,

for their support and for their understanding. I don't say thank you often enough, so I'll say it now. Thank you.

MOONLIGHT RHAPSODY

CHAPTER
One

SHE WOULD BE distant and polite and reasonable, Lacy decided. Courteously friendly, maybe. Nothing more than that. She would not—*would not*—say something bitter and make a complete fool of herself.

Having determined that, Lacy got out of the cab at the darkened concert hall, paid the driver, and walked around to the stage door. The door, to her surprise, was both unguarded and unlocked, so she opened it and stepped inside. No guard there, either.

Where were Randall's watchdogs? True, genius often walked alone, but Randall St. James never had. Where were his helpful minions—the group of managers, publicity people, technicians, and bodyguards she had ruefully dubbed the "Musical Mafia" during that last tour of Europe? Surely he wasn't planning to make his next tour with only a translator in tow. Well, that was *his* business now, she reminded herself. Or it would be as

1

soon as they'd dismissed the possiblity that *she* might be that translator.

Hesitating just inside the door, Lacy allowed her mind to range back briefly to a time many months ago. She remembered Randall's baffled annoyance on discovering that she'd unplugged their phone or coached the doorman not to allow anyone up. She shook her head. He hadn't understood then, and six months wouldn't have changed him much, she knew.

Unfortunately, not much else had changed, either. She held her hands out in front of her and stared at them. They were shaking, just as they used to whenever she heard his step or his voice. Back then it had been from excitement and anticipation. What was it now? And why was her heart thudding just because she was going to see him again for the first time in six months? She didn't want to think about it. She'd put her feelings for Randall behind her, hadn't she?

Taking a deep breath, she headed for the stage. The sound of piano music halted her steps for a moment, but Lacy took a stern hold of herself and walked on. Moving almost silently, she climbed the few steps to the stage and stood in the shadows, watching the absorbed figure seated at a grand piano several yards away.

Her first thought was that he looked so tired. He was also thinner than she remembered, and he'd had his night-black hair cut to a more fashionable length. His coat was discarded on a nearby stool, and his white shirt, open nearly to his waist, exposed the black hair curling on his chest.

Lacy took another deep breath to steady her nerves. Then she realized that either his concentration was fragmented for some reason or he was every bit as tired as he looked, because he broke off in the middle of a difficult passage to swear softly and begin massaging his hands.

Knowing it was useless to postpone the inevitable, Lacy tucked her purse under her arm, jammed her hands into the pockets of her jacket, and slowly walked forward into the light. She wondered if her face reflected the strain she was feeling. She wondered if he could hear the frantic beating of her heart. Most of all, she wondered what he would say to her. After all, this would be the first time they'd spoken since her abrupt move to the East Coast had effectively ended his barrage of unanswered phone calls.

Randall saw her immediately, his tawny gaze following her as she approached the piano. She though she saw some emotion flare deep in the golden depths, but whatever it was, it disappeared too quickly for her to identify it. He said nothing until she reached the piano, his eyes skimming over her silk dress and fur jacket. Then he said simply, "Hello, Lacy. You're looking as beautiful as ever, I see."

Feeling oddly let down, Lacy halted beside the piano and met his gaze. He hadn't even expressed surprise that she was the translator her boss had sent to discuss Randall's upcoming European tour. "Randall," she acknowledged. Nodding toward the piano and affecting a calm she didn't feel, she continued, "Something wrong with the instrument?"

"No." He shrugged slightly. "With me, apparently. I can't get the passage right. As many times as I've played it, too."

The touch of wry humor in his deep voice surprised Lacy. This wasn't the Randall she remembered! Where was his temperamental outburst, his railing at himself for not being perfect? She wet her lips nervously and murmured, "It sounded all right to me."

Randall shook his head. "It wasn't. Sit down over there and listen again; tell me what I'm doing wrong."

Lacy automatically started to obey the command— suggestion or request it certainly wasn't— and then felt a flash of temper. Remaining exactly where she was, she lifted a haughty brow.

Randall watched her for a moment, and then an amused gleam entered his eyes. "Pardon me. Would you *please* sit over there and tell me what I'm doing wrong, Miss Hamilton?"

She walked over to the stool, lifted his coat, and sat down with it in her lap. "Happy to oblige," she said, simultaneously wondering how on earth she was managing this studied nonchalance. "But I'm not in your class, you know," she added.

He looked straight at her, his golden eyes and half smile setting her pulse racing again. "But your technique was always superb."

Lacy shook her head but said nothing. She wasn't about to point out that there was a vast difference between a world-class pianist and one who simply played the piano. Nor was she about to respond to what might or might not have been the innuendo in his words.

Randall studied her curiously for a moment, then turned his attention back to the difficult passage. As she stared at his broad shoulders, he played it through again, and this time Lacy heard the mistakes—three of them. It shook her oddly. She'd listened to him play that piece many times months ago, and never had it been anything but brilliant.

"Well?" he asked, half turning to look at her.

Somehow she couldn't bring herself to point out the

mistakes. "Maybe you've been practicing too much," she suggested.

He stared at her, his lips quirking in a faint smile that let her know he'd noted her reluctance to criticize him. "It's more likely that I haven't practiced *enough*. Friday winds up a national tour, and—"

"You're planning to run this European tour right in on the heels of another one?" she asked incredulously before she could stop herself.

He seemed amused. "The dates of the European tour aren't firmly set yet. It doesn't exactly have to start tomorrow. Besides, I'm tough. I can take it."

Lacy frowned at him, momentarily ignoring the fact that if the dates weren't set yet, her presence wasn't really required. "That's a good way to kill yourself," she retorted irritably.

"Would you care, Lacy?" he asked softly.

She decided to ignore the question. Going on firmly, she said, "Concertizing takes a peak level of health and concentration; you should know that if anybody does. You'll burn yourself out before you're forty and end up teaching piano to a bunch of bored kids."

"Do you think that's likely?"

Lacy sighed. "No" she said truthfully. "You'd probably become a composer and startle the world all over again."

He looked surprised. In an odd tone he said, "Sounds like you have a pretty inflated opinion of my abilities, Lacy."

It was her turn to look surprised. She thought of the driven man she'd known months ago, the man who'd been complex almost beyond her understanding. The brooding silences and temperamental storms. The fierce, demanding passion in him, as unfathomable as the black moods.

She forcibly shoved the memory of passion aside. "You're a world-class pianist, Randall—one of only a handful this country has produced. No one has to tell me what level of 'ability' that takes."

Randall turned on the bench and leaned forward, his elbows on his knees, his hands loosely clasped. The golden eyes were intense, and there was a vulnerablity in his expression that she'd never seen before. In a low voice that cracked slightly, he told her, "There's something wrong, Lacy. There's something missing now. My performances have been...off somehow. And I don't know what's wrong."

Staring into his beautiful eyes, Lacy suddenly sensed that he was reaching out to her. Her heart gave a leap, and she had to remind herself desperately that she wasn't going to let herself start caring about him again. Clutching the coat in her lap, she murmured uneasily, "You're tired, that's all."

He laughed harshly. "You heard me play, Lacy; I've been making the same stupid mistakes for a long time. For months."

Could it be true? she wondered. Possibly. She'd assiduously avoided reading any reviews of his performances, not wanting any reminders of the pain she'd experienced on leaving him. She felt her fingernails bite into her palms, and she made a conscious effort to relax. "Maybe you need a vacation," she offered.

"Maybe." All at once he sounded drained, and the golden eyes looked bleak and remote. Straightening and flexing his shoulders wearily, he murmured, "Have dinner with me, Lacy. Please. I don't want to be alone right now."

It was an open appeal, and her resolve to remain unconcerned wasn't proof against it. It was disarming, because Randall wasn't a man to lean on others. And it was disarming because he seemed so terribly worn.

Her plan to be distant and aloof forgotten, Lacy frowned at him worriedly. "All right." She slipped from the stool and handed his jacket to him as he got to his feet. "How long has it been since you've eaten?" she demanded.

"I don't know." He shrugged into the jacket and buttoned his shirt, robbing her of the view of his masculine chest. She breathed a little easier. "Yesterday, I think."

There was no trace of the old impatience in his voice at being mother-henned, and Lacy felt her worry increase. Randall had always tended to lose himself in his music, forgetting such irrelevant matters as food and rest. It had been she, with a service brat's punctual training, who had insisted on regular hours and meals during the few months they'd shared.

He reached out suddenly to touch the feathered ends of her short black hair. "You've cut it," he murmured, not as though he'd just noticed, but as though he'd been contemplating mentioning it.

She remembered darkened rooms and a deep, caressing voice telling her that her waist-length hair was better than worry beads, and she shivered now as the warmth of his fingers touched her neck. She wondered wildly why the touch of this man—and only this man—should produce such reckless longings in her. Pushing the panicked thought aside, she managed to respond with some measure of composure. "I got tired of the length. This way, it's easier to care for."

Randall must have felt her response to his touch; she sensed his awareness in the familiar yet always startling electric tension between them. And despair washed over her because she realized then that nothing—absolutely nothing—had changed in the march of time.

His peculiar golden eyes stared at her intensely for a moment before his eyelids dropped to hide his expression. "It probably is," he agreed, taking her arm and leading her toward the stage door. He said nothing else until they were in a cab, and then it was only to ask where she wanted to eat.

Lacy named a quiet Italian restaurant across town, thinking that pasta would be the most filling thing for him to eat. She watched as he leaned forward to tell the driver, then winced when Randall read her thoughts with uncanny accuracy.

"Trying to fatten me up, Lacy?" he asked dryly as he settled back beside her.

"You have lost weight," she managed lightly.

"So have you."

"I've been busy." Determined to change the subject, she latched on to her reason for coming to see him. "About this European tour of yours, Randall—Andrew Preston expects me to be your translator, since I was once before and—"

"I know," Randall interrupted calmly.

"You know?" She turned to stare at him. "You mean you— how long have you known?"

"Since I called to let him know when I'd be in town. I reminded him that you were the best he had and asked him to send you along to talk to me. I certainly wasn't arrogant enough to think you'd just drop in to visit me while I practiced. Particularly not after all the trouble you'd gone to to get away from me," he added ruefully.

Feeling oddly off-balance, Lacy asked incredulously,

"You mean you planned all this?"

"I jumped at the chance to see you," he responded grimly.

She knew she should be furious that he'd tricked her into this meeting, but anger wasn't forthcoming. The gritty emotion in his voice starlted her, and her heart jumped into a jungle-drum rhythm again. She swallowed hard and tried to concentrate. "It's impossible, Randall; you must see that," she said tightly, staring straight ahead. "I only came because Andrew insisted, and I didn't want to explain our past . . . relationship to him. But I assumed that once we met you'd instantly agree it was inappropriate and would come up with a reason for asking Andrew for a replacement."

"Why do you think it would be inappropriate, Lacy?" He leaned his head back against the seat and closed his eyes wearily. "I think it would be terribly appropriate. After all, it was on a European tour that you first got into my heart . . . and my bed."

She cast a startled glance toward the cab driver and saw the corner of his mouth twitch. "Dammit, Randall!" she hissed, all too aware of the cabbie's listening ears. "You—you'll have to find another translator."

"I want you," he said flatly. At her audible gasp he continued more seriously, "You're the best translator I've ever worked with; you did a terrific job for me last fall."

"Randall, I—"

"Can't we talk about this over dinner, Lacy?" he asked tiredly, his eyes still closed.

Responding instinctively to the weariness in his voice, and mollified that he'd quickly abandoned the hint of rekindling their past intimacy, she fell silent. Though still worried about the possibility of having to spend several weeks with Randall in Europe in the near future, right now she was more concerned about his state of mind. Again she was painfully aware that nothing had changed—neither Randall and his inattention to her fears, nor she and her feelings for him.

Traitorously, her mind flashed images of some of their happy times together, and she winced at their potency. She pushed memories of precious hours with him aside and determinedly replaced them with memories of the interruptions, of the demands his career made on them and their privacy. The glitter of charity functions and elite parties, the hectic pace of tours.

She forced herself to remember the multitude of small blows that had finally shattered her patience. The intrusion of the "Musical Mafia," the hounding of society press hot on the scent of a famous bachelor's new romance, the demands of Randall to lend his patronage to one function or another, and the glitter of a world in which she felt uncomfortable.

She made herself remember all those things. But it didn't help. The man slumped in the seat beside her still had the power to tug on her heartstrings and set her body alight with need. And that combination, she very much feared, would yank her back into his world whether she willed it or not.

Once at the restaurant and seated at a table, she allowed herself to study him more carefully, watching as he ordered wine to accompany their meal, listening to his deep voice.

What was she expecting to find? His face was still classically handsome, dark and brooding and holding its secrets well. Intense gold eyes still gazed out from between lashes so long any woman would have given her soul for them. He was, as she'd noticed, thinner and tired-looking, but that seemed to be the only difference in him.

"Lacy?"

She blinked, found his questioning gaze on her, and quickly related her choice for the meal. She handed her menu back to the waiter and watched the man walk away, more to avoid Randall's brooding look than anything else.

"Lacy, why did you leave me?" he asked suddenly.

Startled, her gaze flew back to meet his. "You know why."

"I don't think I do, really." He reached for a bread-stick, snapping it evenly in half and staring down at the ends. "I know you weren't happy about that three-city tour. I know you refused to come with me when I asked you. And I know the press badgered you while I was gone. But that's all I really know, Lacy." His gaze lifted, probing, questioning. "When I came home, everything seemed fine—for about ten minutes. Then all hell broke loose, and you were packing and storming out, and you never spoke to me again."

"And what broke all hell loose?" she asked flatly.

"I don't know, dammit! Jake called, and then—"

"Yes," she interrupted tautly, "Jake called. Ten minutes after dropping you off at the apartment, he had to call you. Your manager—agent, whatever you called him—had to phone because he'd gotten home and opened his mail, discovering an invitation for you to perform at yet another fund-raiser."

"Lacy, he's my business manager," Randall said patiently. "It's his job to arrange bookings."

"Yes, it's his job." Her voice was steady, toneless with the effort of keeping anger out of it. "And he did it very well. He kept you so booked up that he begrudged me even a single night alone with you."

"That's not true," Randall grumbled, clearly holding on to his own temper.

Nothing had changed, she reflected bitterly. Randall was still baffled by her contention that his career was bigger than both of them.

"Isn't it?" Lacy struggled to come at the old argument from a fresh viewpoint, a new angle. She momentarily wondered why it was so important that he understand now, when he never had before, but she dismissed the thought. "Randall, you've lived with your career for thirty years. I lived with it for four months. The first few weeks were fine; we were in Europe, we were falling in love, and I was your translator. It was new to me and exciting, and I performed a vital function in your career. Then we went back to your apartment in San Francisco, supposedly to make a life together."

She reached for a breadstick and began snapping it into neat little sections, watching her hands. "I tried to live in your world. I really tried. I went to the chic parties and the charity functions. I listened to snide comments from debs and their high-society mothers. I listened to you practice, and I stood backstage during concerts. I even learned to ignore insulting questions from reporters."

"Lacy—"

"But I never learned to cope with the constant demands," she interrupted fiercely. "On you, on your time— on us. Someone was always calling on the phone or 'dropping in' for a visit to discuss plans with you. I couldn't breathe, Randall. And when Jake called that night—your first night home after being gone two weeks—to tell you something he could have damn well waited at least until morning to tell you—that was it. It was the last straw."

Randall stared at her, still clearly baffled. "Dammit, Lacy, other men have demanding careers. What was I supposed to do? Quit?"

She shook her head, suddenly feeling as tired as he looked. How to make him understand? "Other men have demanding careers," she agreed quietly. "And other women cope with them. But your career is different, Randall. It's totally contained in its own neat little world. And it's a small world, a world of gloss and glitter. Outsiders aren't welcome." Her smile felt twisted. "I could have taken simply being unwelcome. I might even have learned to fit in."

"What are you talking about?" he asked roughly.

"I'm talking about a highbrow, sophisticated society—the society that peoples your world."

"That's nothing but reverse snobbery!"

"No, that's reality." She lifted her eyes to stare at him levelly. "I'm an Air Force brat, Randall. I've been dragged around the globe since I was born. Lord knows I'm at home in a lot of situations, but your world defeated me." She hesitated briefly. "If we could have escaped from that world from time to time . . . But we never could. And I just couldn't take it anymore!"

After her outburst, both of them fell silent. The food arrived, but neither of them did justice to the meal. Randall drank more wine than anything else, and Lacy felt a prickling of uneasiness when he ordered another bottle.

His moody expression defied her to make some comment, and, unwilling to make a scene, she said nothing.

By the time they rose to leave, Randall was unsteady on his feet, and his eyes wore the hard glitter of raw gold. He leaned heavily on Lacy as they left the restaurant, his arm draped around her shoulder and his hand uncomfortably close to the swell of her breast. Torn between worry, irritation, and the vague suspicion that something was off-center, Lacy practically pushed him into a cab and then climbed in after him.

"Where to, Miss?" The driver obviously realized that Randall was in no condition to direct him.

Lacy stared at Randall as he sat slumped in the seat, his eyes closed, then sighed and gave the driver her address. As she sat back, Randall slid a little sideways, his head coming to rest on her shoulder. Still reluctant to make a scene, she didn't push him away, but she swore silently when his hand came to rest on her upper thigh. Carefully, she moved his hand, and he muttered something indistinguishable in her ear.

What in heaven's name was she supposed to do now? She could hardly send Randall back to his hotel alone— not in the state he was in. And if anyone from the press saw him in this condition, it could have a serious effect on his career.

And most of his career was still ahead of him; he was only thirty-five. Unless Randall was truly losing that indefinable quality that made him stand out from the rest, as his statement about "something being wrong" implied. If that were true, bad press would only hasten the downward slide.

Lacy shuddered. Why had he told her that? Damn him, why had he told her? She didn't want to care what happened to him, yet somehow he'd made her care. Or perhaps she'd just never stopped caring.

Either way, she couldn't abandon him now.

CHAPTER
Two

WHEN THE CAB reached her apartment building, Lacy
paid the driver and gratefully accepted his offer of help
in getting her escort up to her apartment. It was an em-
barrassing situation, to say the least, but by then she was
too concerned about Randall to worry much about it.
Between the two of them, they managed to get him up
the stairs and onto the couch in her apartment. She thanked
the driver and smiled slightly as she closed the door
behind him. And people said you could never find help
in New York City!

She stripped off her jacket and dropped it and her
purse onto a chair, then turned to regard Randall's slumped
form. The couch was a long one, thank heavens, and he
probably wouldn't be too uncomfortable on it for the
night. But his jacket should come off. *That* turned out

to be a major problem, complicated by the fact that he was no help at all. It took ten minutes and some peculiar contortions, but she finally got the binding garment off.

By the time Randall seemed fairly comfortable, Lacy was hot, tired, and irritably amused about the situation. Leaving him to sleep off the effects of the wine, she went into her bedroom to change. She decided to take a quick shower, and half an hour later, wearing a zip-up floor-length robe, she emerged from her bedroom to find her guest still sleeping soundly.

She curled up in a chair near the couch, an unopened book in her lap, and stared at him. The Randall she remembered rarely drank, and never to excess, but she wondered if his worry over the possible loss of his talent had caused him to drink more often lately. He had always seemed so strong! Was the problem as serious as he seemed to think, or had Randall simply been working too hard? And how could she help?

As soon as that question occurred to her, Lacy winced. She couldn't get involved with Randall again. Not again. Their conversation at dinner should have shown her clearly that Randall would never understand why their relationship had failed. He'd lived in his rarefied world too long, she thought, to realize that it was an entity apart from that of mere mortals. From child prodigy to adult genius, he'd known no other life, no other way. He was neither blind nor insensitive, she knew; it was only that a lifetime's experience wasn't a thing to be easily set aside.

No, she couldn't get involved with him again. Not with him and not with his world. She hadn't been born to that world, and she mistrusted its false glitter. So, tomorrow morning she'd send him on his way. She'd tell her employer she refused to translate for Randall St.

James, and if Andrew balked, she'd quit. Translators were always in demand; if necessary, she could find a job abroad.

She wouldn't get involved with him again.

That resolution disappeared from her mind when Randall stirred slightly on the couch and groaned softly. He looked feverish, and Lacy put her book aside and slipped from her chair to move over and sit on the edge of the couch. "Randall?" In almost a detached manner she watched her hand reach out to brush a lock of his dark hair away from his proud forehead. His eyes opened, the golden depths cloudy as he stared up at her.

"Lacy? What happened?" he asked thickly.

"You passed out," she told him dryly. "I decided to let you sleep it off on my couch."

"Oh. Sorry." He reached up to rub his forehead blearily, and when his hand dropped it somehow wound up on her shoulder. His fingers moved almost absently, and Lacy felt the heat of them through the thin terry of her robe. She started to pull away, completely forgetting the laws of gravity, which insisted that his hand would move downward. She gasped when his hand closed over her breast, feeling her body betray her as the nipple rose tautly against his palm.

Randall's eyes immediately darkened, and with a smothered sound he suddenly pulled her down on top of him. Off guard and off-balance, Lacy didn't stand a chance.

"I've been wanting to do this ever since you walked across the stage," he murmured huskily.

Lacy felt his hand on the nape of her neck, pulling her inexorably down, and before she could even gasp in protest, his lips were on hers. Memories, long suppressed, surged into her mind like an ocean's tide, but the memories were overpowered by the raw, searing hunger of his kiss.

It was like nothing she had ever experienced before, nothing she would have believed possible. She had never felt such stark, unhidden need in a man. His tongue invaded her mouth in a virtual act of possession, and Lacy's weak, instinctive resistance shattered. Fire licked along her nerve endings, ran through her veins, and she tore her lips from his in a last desperate bid for sanity.

"No! Randall, don't! You—"

"Don't stop me, Lacy." He shifted abruptly, and she was beside him on the wide couch. "Don't do that to me." There was something bleak and hurting in the darkened depths of his golden eyes. "I need you so badly."

She stared at him as he rose on an elbow to gaze down at her, and when his hand moved to the front zipper of her robe, she was helpless to stop him. The lamp by the couch cast a soft glow over her milky flesh when he parted the robe. Lacy drew a deep, shaken breath, and he groaned softly as he stared down at her. "Oh, Lord, you're beautiful!" His lips moved to possess what his hands had exposed.

As if she were one of his pianos, he had tuned her body to respond only to his touch. No other man had ever been able to rouse this wild, reckless response in her, and her hands moved of their own volition to tangle in the hair at his nape.

She forgot her resolution to avoid any involvement with this man, forgot the unbearable heartache their parting had brought her. She wanted to feel his hands and lips on her body, and every other consideration faded before that one inescapable need.

His tongue was moving sensuously around her nipple, his hand sliding down over her flat, quivering stomach, and Lacy bit her lip as fiery sensations flooded her body. She wanted to cry out to him to stop what he was doing, to never stop, to join her in this enchanted world he had created, but the only sound that escaped her trembling lips was a moan of pleasure.

Suddenly desperate to touch him, she fumbled with the remaining buttons of his shirt and felt a shudder wrack his body.

"Yes . . . touch me," he muttered hoarsely. "I need to feel your hands on me, Lacy. It's been so long!"

Impatiently pushing the shirt off his shoulders, Lacy was only vaguely aware when he shrugged it off and flung it to the floor. She raked her fingernails gently down his chest, finding the flat male nipples and tugging slightly.

With a throaty laugh he murmured, "You've become a wildcat. My own little wildcat. Oh, Lacy!"

Her fingers continued their exploration, sliding down his hard stomach and making a tiny, teasing foray beneath the belt of his slacks. His groan of pleasure only spurred her on. Her hands moved over his lean ribs, explored the muscled strength of his back, darted down to probe the base of his spine. She felt one of his legs trap her restless ones, and she moaned again when his hands came dangerously close to the very heart of her desire.

He pulled her suddenly, fiercely against him, as if he would mold every inch of her body against his, and Lacy felt the hard heat of the desire he made no effort to hide.

"Let me love you, darling," he growled huskily against her lips. "I need you so badly tonight."

Something that had been tapping insistently at the back

of Lacy's mind broke through at his words. *Tonight*. He needed her... *tonight*. Why? To prove to himself that the possible loss of his musical gifts wouldn't make him less of a man?

With an effort that felt as though it broke something inside her, she pushed against his chest and asked unsteadily, "Is it me you need, Randall? Or would any woman do?"

"What are you talking about?" he asked hoarsely, his eyes still clouded as he lifted his head to stare down at her.

Trying to gather her thoughts, she said gently, "You're feeling very unsure of yourself, worried about losing your music."

"And I'm trying to prove myself—is that what you're saying?" The golden eyes were slowly clearing of passion, but the gathering storm there made her nervous, as did his even voice.

"Aren't you?"

"What I'm doing," he said very slowly and distinctly, "is making love to my woman."

Astonished at the utter possessiveness of his statement, she said a little wildly, "I'm not your woman!"

"But you are." He was smiling, a peculiarly predatory sort of smile. "You've been my woman since the day we met. What's more, you know it. And I'll get you to admit it if it's the last thing I ever do!"

"No!" She pushed frantically against his chest, turning her head away as his lips sought hers. "Dammit, I don't belong to you! I'm not a piece of property!"

A sudden suspicion crystallized in her mind, giving her the strength to shove him away. It was she who landed in a very undignified heap on the carpet, and she hastily zipped her robe before turning to stare at him. With awful calm she said, "You're not drunk."

Randall rested his head against the low arm of the couch and smiled at her, laughter dancing in his eyes. "Those who know me best," he admitted, "claim I could put the whole Russian army under the table drinking nothing but vodka on an empty stomach. The wine didn't even make a dent."

"And I fell for it," she said dazedly, staring at the unscrupulous fiend on her couch. "I fell for it hook, line, and sinker. That makes twice in one day. My Lord—I even felt sorry for you!"

"Was that why you responded to me so delightfully?" he asked with interest.

Lacy felt a flush stain her cheeks. "Get out of here!" she ordered, struggling to her feet.

Randall calmly linked his hands together behind his head. "Not a chance. I'm here, and here I'll stay."

She stared at him blankly until a sudden sense of outrage sparked her wits. "You're out of your mind!" she yelped. "You really expect to come crashing back into my life like a—a—"

"Lover?" he supplied helpfully.

"I can think of a better word!" she retorted, glaring at him. "Look, Randall, whatever you've got in mind, you can just forget it! I'm not in the market for a lover, thank you very much, and I wouldn't choose you even if I were!"

"But I choose you," he told her calmly. "Chose you, in fact, from the very beginning. And I'm a very determined man, Lacy. In spite of the way you ran out on me—"

"Ran out on you?" Lacy ran a hand through her short

hair and stared at him. "Randall, I left—period. What was between us ended!"

"No."

"Yes! Dammit, didn't you hear anything I said to you tonight? The wall between us might as well be the Berlin Wall, because neither of us is ever going to cross it!"

"No wall stands forever," he argued.

"This one will." She tried to marshal her thoughts. "Randall, you're a gifted musician, and you belong in your world. But I belong in mine."

"You keep talking as if we live on separate planets," he muttered, clearly frustrated by the argument.

"We might as well," she said, hearing the despair in her own voice.

"But we don't!" he snapped. "Lacy, I'm trying to understand how you feel. I really am. Stop talking about worlds and tell me the problems—the real, concrete problems."

He sat up and gazed at her, waiting, expectant. Lacy sat down on the low arm of the couch, wondering why she was even bothering. But she knew why, deep down inside. It was because those few moments on the couch with him had reminded her of what she had given up. And how many people were granted a second chance after losing something precious? She had to try. Somehow, she had to try.

"The problems," he prompted quietly.

"I can't stand glittering social 'events,'" she said finally. "Meaningless conversation, too much to drink, and complete unreality. You're asked to attend that type of thing a dozen times a month."

"I can send my regrets," he said immediately.

She shook her head. "Jake would have a fit. Remember visibility, Randall. In your career, one must be visible."

"I'll be visible on stage," he returned flatly. "Unless, of course, the concerts are a problem."

Lacey felt her temper flare, and she glared at him. "If you're trying to be funny, I'm not in the mood!"

Randall looked honestly surprised. "I wasn't. If the concerts are a problem, we'll have to face it, won't we?"

"And if I couldn't live with the concerts?" she challenged.

He looked at her steadily. "If you asked me to give up performing, I'd do it."

Deeply shaken, Lacy swallowed hard. She was bewildered by the certainty in his voice. Could he possibly care more about her than his music? No. No, it didn't make sense! "I'd never ask you to do that," she managed weakly.

Randall smiled suddenly, a crooked, strangely endearing smile. "Since I know you'd never ask, I can't prove it, but I would stop the concerts if you asked."

Lacy hastily shunted the subject aside; she didn't want to think about what his offer meant. "It's not the concerts—it's everything that goes with them. Your retinue, for instance. I can't—"

"No more retinue." He laughed. "No more Musical Mafia. I disbanded them."

"Why?" She stared at him. "The technicians, the bodyguards? Especially the bodyguards; Randall, there was a threat on your life."

He shrugged. "There were never any attempts." Suddenly wry, he added, "Besides, you were always laughing at them. I just realized that the whole thing was ridiculous."

A little wry herself, Lacy noted silently that she'd gotten through to him on something, at least. "Not laughing at them. They were just so solemn! And they never seemed to *do* anything. They just looked stoically through people, and I hated feeling invisible."

Randall grinned faintly. "Was that why you were always trying to break them up, the way tourists do to the guards at Buckingham Palace?"

Lacy giggled in spite of herself. "Like the time I got them involved in a ridiculous discussion over which came first—the chicken or the egg. I thought Alan was going to blow a fuse."

Still smiling, Randall murmured, "You made him laugh, anyway. You made us all laugh, Lacy."

She moved suddenly, as though to throw off an unwelcome hand. "Nothing's really changed, Randall. Retinue or no, no one can change that much in just six months."

"How can you be so sure?" he asked insistently. When she failed to reply, he added, "Can you deny that what we had was fantastic, Lacy?"

"That doesn't mean it would be again," she countered, reaching for straws and finding a flimsy one.

"Oh, no?" He glanced pointedly down at the couch where they had lain together only moments before, then lifted a curiously glittering gaze to her face.

Lacy flushed. "If you were a gentleman—" she began in a treacherously unsteady voice.

"But I'm not. And I'll do whatever I have to do to get you back into my bed, where you belong."

She felt her senses reel. Dear Lord, he hadn't been this possessive when they'd been together before! She tried vaguely to understand the urgent note in his voice, the urgency in his eyes, but failed. It was desire, of course, but it was something else, too, and she didn't know what. "No," she managed at last, her voice as unsteady as before.

"Yes," he told her, his tone the still, waiting quiet of nature just before a hurricane.

"I won't go through it all again," she told him flatly.

Randall stared at her. "What about what I went through?" he asked, the words dropping between them like stones.

"I don't know what you mean," she said evenly.

"I mean do you care what I went through when you left me," he elaborated. "Doesn't that matter to you, Lacy?"

She didn't want it to matter. She wanted to tell him to leave and be done with it. With all of it. But his weary, strained face and the appeal in his eyes defeated her.

Slowly she managed, "I'm sorry if I hurt you, Randall. But I had no choice, and that's something you'll never understand. Can't we just leave it at that? Let it end?"

"No." He raked a hand through his hair, the gesture clear evidence of his disturbed emotions. "Lacy, you never really told me what was wrong while we were together. You just threw everything in my face at the last minute and left me. In all fairness, I deserve another chance."

"Why?" She held his eyes with her own, needing desperately to know why he was so insistent on another chance for them. "Why does it matter now, Randall?"

"It matters because I need you." He slid over on the couch and patted the cushion beside him. "Sit here, Lacy, please. Hear me out."

After a moment, Lacy rose from the arm of the couch

and sat down beside him. But she shored up her resolve firmly; no matter what he said, she wouldn't weaken. She wouldn't!

"All right, Randall. I'm listening. But I don't think you'll convince me that anything's changed."

"Everything's changed!" He looked at her with restless eyes. "Lacy, something happened when you came into my life. I don't know what it was. I've gone over those months again and again. What was different? The only answer is that you were there.

"You opened my eyes somehow. There was nothing false or glittery about you. You were real, completely honest in your response to what went on around you." He hesitated for a moment, watching her with those searching eyes.

And when he went on, his voice roughened. "Then you were gone, and everything was wrong. Something vital was missing, from my life and from my music. Lacy, for nearly thirty years I've always known where I stood with my music; I've known whether it was good, bad, or indifferent.

"But I don't know that any longer! I look at it, and I can't see it clearly. The music's changing—or I am. And after thirty years,"—his smile was twisted, pained— "I'm not so sure I like it."

Lacy moved uneasily. "Then why ask for more trouble?" she asked. "Why open everything up all over again? Randall, you're at an age when your music would begin to change, mature, naturally. That's all it is. It has nothing to do with me."

"Hasn't it?" He shook his head abruptly. "Dammit, I don't know how to make you understand! Lacy, I need you." The golden eyes gazed into hers with an intensity she found hard to face. "I need you! I won't walk out that door and let it end. We were together for four months, and I can't believe that was enough time to work out the problems."

"Randall—"

"At least give me the chance to show you how the music's changed," he interrupted quickly. "Lacy, you heard me play tonight; you heard the stupid mistakes. And you know that everything in my personal life affects the music; my concentration's been shot all to hell since you left."

"It can't be that bad," she objected weakly, but the strain on his face was pulling at her heart again.

With a faint lift of his brow, he said wryly, "Need convincing, eh? All right. Come to the concert Friday night. If you don't agree that something's gone badly wrong, we'll go our separate ways again with no arguments from me. Agreed?"

"Agreed," she heard herself saying. Lacy was very sure of one thing: Randall would never —*never*—deliberately wreck a performance. He just wouldn't. It would be like cutting himself with a knife.

"And until then," he went on quietly, "will you give me another chance? A chance to prove to you that the— the wall between us doesn't have to stand forever? A chance to show you how much I need you—for me, personally, and never mind the music or the tour? Will you give me that chance, Lacy?"

She bit her lip indecisively for a moment, then nodded reluctantly. Her sense of fairness forced her to agree that she had really given him no chance the last time to work out the problems. But it was more than that. Desire still throbbed through her veins after the interlude on the couch. And the pleading in the eyes of a man who had never, to her knowledge, pleaded for anything in his life had defeated her.

It had been an afternoon and evening of surprises, strong emotions, and bargains, and Lacy was tired. She was even more tired when a glance at the clock told her it was midnight. And Randall looked weary. Weary and vulnerable and somehow drained. She didn't have the heart to send him back to his hotel.

She rose to her feet, both grateful and unnerved when he made no move to stop her. "It's late, Randall. You can take the spare bedroom for tonight. It'll save you the long ride back to your hotel," she ended lamely.

Gratitude flickered in his eyes as he nodded and leaned forward to get his shirt from the floor before rising. "Thank you, Lacy." He hesitated for a moment, then asked, "Your roommate? There were two names on your mailbox downstairs."

Lacy remembered somewhat bitterly the struggle she and the cabbie had had lugging Randall's supposedly unconscious form up the four flights to her apartment. The next time he pretended to be totally plastered, she'd leave him where he fell!

"My roommate got married last month; I haven't had time to take her name off the box," she managed calmly. When he nodded again, she said, "First door on the right. The bathroom's at the end of the hall."

He started forward but stopped just inside the hallway and looked back at her. "You're sure you don't want company in your bed tonight?" he teased.

She frowned at him. "Positive. Go to bed, Randall. You're dead on your feet."

He gave her an odd smile, murmured a quiet good

night, and went on down the hall.

Lacy stood where she was, absently shoving her hands into the pockets of her robe. Had he seriously thought they could settle everything simply by going to bed together? After the events of the day, she was too confused to think straight about anything.

She had until Friday to sort things out in her mind. And if Randall played as brilliantly as she expected him to, it wouldn't matter anyway.

As usual, Lacy woke instantly at the time she'd mentally set for herself the night before. It was a soldier's faculty—waking at any hour she chose—and a carry-over from all the childhood mornings of lying in her bed and listening to reveille. She had amused herself during those days by attempting to wake herself up shortly before the bugle. The habit stuck with her.

A glance at the decorative clock on her nightstand told her that she'd hit it on the nose this time. Six. And she didn't have to be in the office until eight-thirty. She laced her fingers together behind her head and stared at the ceiling thoughtfully. Seldom one to have a cloudy mind in the morning, she remembered last night quite clearly.

She'd made a deal with Randall.

In retrospect, she decided she'd been more than a little foolish. Why should she let herself in for the certain pain of battering her head against a wall that would never yield? Lacy remembered the passion and need in his touch, and she shivered. That was why. The force of desire between them was elemental and too powerful to be denied. And, as if that weren't enough, the man still had a firm grip on her heart. Damn him.

After six months away from him, she thought she'd nearly gotten him out of her system, and here he was again, working his way back in. Why did his national tour have to end in New York City? She had the awful feeling that getting involved with him a second time would be no less painful than the first, and that reality would slap her in the face just as hard when it was all over again.

Lacy shoved her confusion into a back room of her mind and slammed the door on all of it. Later. She'd think about it later.

She allowed her gaze to wander around her gold and ruby-wine bedroom. The six months in New York was about on a par with the time she usually spent in one city. While she was growing up, home had been wherever her Air Force father had been stationed. And her job had her traveling constantly. But she planned to remain here indefinitely, and so, for the first time, she had turned her apartment into a home.

And she had grown rather fond of it. Elements of her personality were evident in the decor: her collection of glass and porcelain unicorns; the colorful pillows from faraway countries piled neatly along with the bedspread on the Oriental chest at the foot of her bed; the oils and watercolors she'd acquired over the years; her wide selection of books in the living room; even the ridiculous little signs scattered through the apartment, like the one on her bedroom door that read NOTICE—OCCUPANT MAY LOSE CONTROL WITHOUT WARNING! A teasing present from her ex-roommate, that.

With sudden clarity Lacy realized that she was looking around at her cozy, secure little world and feeling decidedly threatened. Why? Randall, of course. He'd slammed back into her life without warning, and she was afraid of what loving him would do to her this time.

Loving him?

Lacy closed her eyes, and a ragged sigh escaped her. Loving him. She would love him again, she knew. Some things went far beyond choice, and love was one of them. Given a choice, Lacy wondered if she would choose to love an uncomplicated man and live an uncomplicated life. A nine-to-five routine, mortgage, two point five kids, and a dog.

And a husband not driven by genius and fame.

Would she choose that? After traveling around the globe for the better part of twenty-six years and seeing things tourists never saw? After having been granted the chance to love a man who was as complex as a multi-faceted diamond—and just as dazzling?

Could she choose less than that now?

Lacy frowned and tried to be reasonable. Sometimes half a loaf was better than no bread, wasn't it? She could be content with less if it meant less pain and struggle. She could!

Still frowning, she slid from her bed. And then she stopped, the mirror on the back of her bedroom door catching her attention.

The woman in the mirror was wearing a peach-colored nightgown over her tall, slim body with its surprisingly full breasts and athletic carriage. Her face was distinctive rather than beautiful, its elfin quality emphasized by slanting jade eyes and gently curved lips. Lacy reached up to touch the short feathered ends of her black hair and saw that those jade eyes were glowing with a hope beyond reason. A hope that all the sensible reasoning in the world wouldn't change.

Sometimes half a loaf *wasn't* better than none . . . Lacy swore softly and went to dress.

CHAPTER
Three

HALF AN HOUR later she walked quietly along the polished hardwood floor of the hall, carrying her shoes so as not to awaken her still-sleeping guest. Once in the kitchen, she approached the neat breakfast bar and rummaged through a drawer until she located an apron to tie over the skirt of her green dress.

She turned on the radio softly to listen to the semiclassical, instrumental music she preferred. Shunning the instant coffee she normally used, she unearthed her percolator, filled it, and spooned in some of the wonderfully rich coffee she'd found in South America. For special occasions. Not that this *was* one, of course.

Ten minutes later the coffee was bubbling merrily and bacon was spitting furiously in the skillet. Lacy was industriously beating eggs in a bowl and singing quietly to herself when she suddenly had the feeling that she was no longer alone. Setting the bowl carefully on the woodgrain counter, she abandoned the rest of her song and turned to look toward the doorway of the kitchen.

Randall, wearing only slacks, was leaning against the jamb, arms folded casually across his bare chest. His golden eyes were unreadable, but his ever-awesome masculine presence took her breath away.

"Good morning." He smiled, his even white teeth flashing briefly. "I didn't want to startle you. You looked so . . . content."

Lacy found that she had nothing to do with her hands, and she hastily shoved them into the pockets of her apron. "Good morning," she murmured, ignoring the rest of his comment.

Randall's gaze moved slowly up from her stockinged feet, sliding over the green dress, the off-white apron bearing the picture of an irritable cat snapping "Don't bother me, I'm cooking!" and on up to the pulse pounding rapidly in her throat. She could feel his eyes on that spot, burning into her, and she was relieved when he finally met her own gaze.

He fingered his blue-shadowed jaw and smiled wryly. "Mind if I borrow your razor?"

"Of course not." Lacy heard her own calm voice and was vaguely surprised. "It's in the cabinet by the vanity in the bathroom. Help yourself. Take a shower if you like." She turned quickly back to her preparations.

It was a full five minutes before she sneaked a peek over her shoulder to be sure he was gone. The tension drained out of her, and she scolded herself sharply for her uneasiness. What was wrong with her, for heaven's sake? Randall wouldn't bite her!

But she was still uneasy. Despite her arguments that nothing had changed, she had to admit that this new Randall with his quiet manner and wry smile was not what she had expected. And she didn't know how to deal with him.

She wondered what had changed him. Randall had never been a vain man; he'd always been so wrapped up in his music that he'd only politely noticed the fame his genius had caused. He had accepted the fame because it was a part of his music.

And the temperamental storms within his personal life had never carried over into his career. Once on a stage, Randall had always been a consummate professional. The public had no idea of the brooding man who raged at himself for not being perfect, the man obsessed by the genius that drove him.

Lacy had seen no glimpse of that man last night or this morning. Somehow, for some reason, he *had* changed. There was nothing in the world more important to Randall than his music. Was *it* changing? Was his talent burning out after thirty years of brilliant success? Was she watching the walls of his strength crumbling? Was this strange, quiet dignity his last refuge from a world that would pity him?

From a woman who would pity him?

She felt a drop of moisture fall to her hand and blotted it with a dish towel. Almost savagely she blotted the others on her cheeks. "Damn you," she whispered huskily. "Damn you, anyway."

By the time Randall had showered, shaved, and dressed, breakfast was ready and Lacy had herself under strict control. She had set the breakfast bar, and now she poured their coffee as Randall took the stool she gestured to.

Surveying the well-prepared and appetizing meal, Randall murmured, "I never knew you could cook."

"You never asked." Lacy busied herself with sitting down across from him and spreading a napkin over her lap. "When we were traveling you called room service." In spite of herself, she added, "When we were home, we usually ate out with 'friends' or business associates."

There was a moment of silence; then Randall said quietly, "I guess that's true. What else don't I know about you, Lacy?"

She lifted her head to meet his eyes. She wanted to strike out at him, to punish him for the jumbled emotions inside her. She wanted desperately to feel nothing for him. But a curious sense of defeat rose within her, and she knew she wouldn't strike out at him. She couldn't.

"Eat your breakfast, Randall." She bent her head and began to eat silently, and after a moment he followed suit.

"I haven't seen a piano around here," he said lightly a few moments later.

"There isn't one."

"Where do you practice?"

"I don't have much time to practice these days, since Andrew moved me to the East Coast. He keeps me busy. When I do want to practice, two of my neighbors have pianos I can use."

Randall looked at her thoughtfully. "You should have gone on competing after you finished college. You're good, Lacy."

Lacy shook her head. "I enjoyed competing when I was a kid," she said, "but I never planned to go on with it. I love music, but I love languages more." She looked at him directly. "And after living in your world for a while, I'm glad I stopped competing."

He winced. "You're still talking about two separate worlds," he objected. "Lacy, I'm made of flesh and blood, and I live in the real world—"

"No, you don't," she interrupted quietly. "Not the real world. Not the one I grew up in. Randall, from the age of five you were insulated from the real world. Your gift made you special. You never had to cope with peer pressure in school; you were tutored. You never had to decide what you'd do with your life; that was obvious all along. In *your* life there were no surprises, no sudden upheavals. Everything was planned and secure. How real does that sound?"

Randall leaned forward slightly, staring at her. "How do you think I felt about that, Lacy? Did you ever stop to think—"

The phone shrilled an interruption.

They stared at each other for a moment, and then Lacy leaned sideways to reach for the kitchen wall phone. With despairing certainty, she knew who would be calling.

"Hello?" Lacy listened to the all-too-familiar voice on the other end and was totally unable to respond to its cheerful tone. "Yes," she murmured flatly in response to his jovial comment. "Yes, it's been a long time. Yes, he's here. Hold on."

She curled her fingers around the mouthpiece and looked steadily at Randall. "It didn't take him long to find you, did it?" she asked tonelessly.

"Jake?" Randall queried tightly.

"Jake." She handed the phone across to him. "Nothing's changed, Randall." Lacy abruptly slid from the stool, tossed her napkin over her plate, picked up her purse and jacket, and slipped her shoes on. "I'm going to work. Leave the dishes; I'll get them later. And make sure the door locks when you leave, would you?" Desperate to get away from him, she headed almost blindly for the door. She heard him say quickly, "Hold on, Jake," and she tried to reach the door before he could stop her.

"Lacy?"

With one hand on the opened door, she paused and looked back at him with all the control she could muster. He was standing only a few feet away and looking at her with an expression she couldn't define to save her life.

"Lacy, I . . . Ah, hell!" He crossed the space between them in two long strides, determination and self-control holding his face rigid. "Since talking doesn't seem to work, maybe something else will!"

She knew what the "something else" would be even before his hand slammed the door closed and his arms caught her close. She knew, and she wished she could hate him for using the one weapon she was helpless to fight. Staring up at his unbearably handsome face for an eternal moment, she almost hated him. But not quite.

"Randall, no!"

"Yes!" His head bent, golden eyes darkening as though dimmed by a falling curtain. "Nothing else matters, Lacy. Nothing but this."

His lips sought hers, found them, possessed them. He kissed her as if he would tear down the wall between them with the very fury of his need. He kissed her with a desperate, scorching hunger that would brook no denial, accept no resistance.

And she couldn't resist. She released her hold on her purse and jacket, allowing them to fall to the floor. Her arms crept up around his neck, her fingers tangling in his glossy black hair. She felt his arms pulling her even closer, the thin fabric of her dress no barrier against the fierce, throbbing desire she could feel in him. Heat swept through her body from head to toe.

How could she fight this? How in heaven's name could she fight it? It was what she wanted, what her body had hungered for for six endless months, and no thread of sanity, no burst of reason, could fight it.

Randall's lips left hers to plunder the sensitive flesh of her throat, and she could feel his ragged breathing and the tremor that shook his lean frame. Both sent an answering shudder through her body.

"Lacy," he muttered hoarsely. "Don't you see that what we have is special? We can't let anything destroy that—anything! We can work it out, whatever it takes. Just don't throw it away again without giving me another chance!"

Her eyelids lifted slowly, heavy with the weight of desire, and she looked over his shoulder. Just barely visible was the telephone receiver, lying on the breakfast bar where he'd left it. The phone—and the demands of his world.

Sanity won out this time, giving Lacy the strength to disentangle herself from his embrace. She bent and retrieved her purse and jacket, then straightened and met his gaze.

Harshly, his face still stormy, Randall said, "You still want me, Lacy. Don't deny it."

"I won't deny it," she responded tonelessly. "That hasn't changed. But neither has much else. Jake's waiting for you, Randall."

"To hell with Jake!" he snapped violently.

She smiled ruefully. "I've wished him there a few times myself. Poor Jake." She straightened her shoulders. "I have to go to work."

"Lacy!" He sounded almost desperate.

She slipped out the door and closed it softly behind her.

"There's a frantic gleam in those beautiful green eyes," announced a masculine voice from the doorway of her office. Lacy looked up to see the owner of the voice come in and drop into her visitor's chair.

"Look," she began, addressing her boss with a distressing lack of respect, "I know I'm studying Japanese, but that doesn't mean I've mastered the language. And if you don't tell the switchboard to stop putting that poor, befuddled Japanese businessman through to me, you can find yourself another translator!"

Andrew Preston's eyebrows shot up toward his thick red hair, and he looked as startled as it was possible for an innately mild man to look. "Hey, hey," he murmured soothingly. "I'll tell the switchboard, Miss Hamilton. Does that smooth your ruffled feathers?"

Lacy tried to get a grip on herself. She'd been growing steadily testier all day and felt now as if she could easily scream, throw something, or burst into tears. It wasn't a comfortable feeling.

"Are you all right?" Andrew asked with real concern in his voice. "I'm told you've been snapping at people all day."

"I'm fine, Andrew. Just a little tired."

"Lacy, what's really wrong?"

She looked up to meet his concerned blue eyes and couldn't help but smile. Andrew and Connie, his wife, had helped to make the past six months bearable. Their uncritical friendship had pulled her out of her shell in spite of herself, though they'd never stretched that friendship with matchmaking. She was grateful for that.

But she couldn't confide in Andrew about Randall. Even in the past, when the press had had a field day with their relationship, she'd convinced Andrew that the coverage was due solely to the fact that Lacy had been the only woman in Randall's entourage, and that the gossip columnists had been grasping at straws. Andrew was too much of a father figure for her to relate intimate details to him. And though he might have suspected something more, Lacy knew, he'd respected her privacy—as people in *her* world were wont to do.

"I'm just tired, Andrew. I'll be fine. Really."

"Don't tell me, then." He grimaced playfully. "I'm a grown man; my feelings don't get bruised that easily."

"Andrew . . ."

"Okay, okay. But look—take the rest of the afternoon off, will you please? Go shopping or something. Connie always feels like a million bucks after a shopping spree. Spends about that much, too."

Lacy smothered a laugh, amused for the first time that day.

Obviously encouraged by her response, Andrew went on, "I mean it; take off. Connie's got her own private connections in this place, you know, and if her source tells her I made you work when you weren't feeling yourself, she'll burn my dinner three nights running."

Lacy laughed and began to gather her things. "I'd hate to be responsible for your indigestion! Consider me gone."

"And don't come back tomorrow if you're not feeling better," he called after her as she left the office.

Lacy went shopping but didn't buy anything. She went to a movie and left halfway through. She went to a museum and ambled about not really seeing anything. After a while, because there was no place else to go, she

went home. She didn't want to go home; she didn't want
to face her empty apartment.

But she discovered when she arrived that it wasn't
quite empty. There was a large vase of peach blossoms
on the coffee table. Lacy touched a delicate bloom. From
the depths of her memory, the meaning of the flowers
surfaced. "My heart is thine," she murmured. She immediately jerked her hand away. Absurd. Randall couldn't
have known what the flowers meant.

Wandering aimlessly around, Lacy discovered that he
had left the apartment very neat. His bed was made, the
dishes washed and put away. There was no sign of his
earlier presence save the flowers. Lacy stared at them
for a while and then went to get out of her work clothes.

Later, having donned a black caftan, she curled up in
front of the television. She pulled her knitting basket to
her and began to work automatically on the scarf she'd
just started, fingers flying with no direction from her
mind.

It was eight o'clock when the doorbell rang. She got
up, put her knitting aside, and turned the television off.
She knew, with an absolute certainty that defied defi-
nition, who was at the door.

And he was.

Randall stood staring gravely down at her, looking
starkly masculine and impossibly appealing. "May I come
in?" he asked quietly.

Silently Lacy stepped back to allow him to enter. Just
as silently she shut the door behind him and led the way
into the living room. She had known. All day she'd
known that he wouldn't be able to leave things as she'd
left them between the two of them this morning.

She sat down in her chair, watching as he restlessly
moved about the room. She grudgingly admired the un-

thinking grace of his movements. Randall wasn't an athlete, but he had always been surprisingly fit for one who spent a great deal of his time sitting on a piano bench. The broad shoulders and finely muscled body spoke of an effort to keep in shape.

"I've been walking," he announced suddenly, pausing in his pacing to gaze out the window.

"Have you?"

"All day." He resumed his pacing. "Should have been practicing, but I didn't. I just walked."

Lacy sighed. "What do you want, Randall?"

He sat down on the arm of the couch, which was at a right angle to her chair, and stared at her for a long moment. "I want us to stop hurting each other, Lacy. Is that too much to ask?"

Lacy kept her face impassive. "I've never tried to hurt you, Randall."

"You hurt me every time you look at me with indifference in your eyes," he said.

She was both surprised and confused, and she hoped none of it showed. "What did you expect? That you could walk back into my life and I'd welcome you with open arms?"

He leaned forward, elbows on his knees as he stared at her intently. "Lacy, when we first met—"

"Do you have to keep dredging up the past?" she asked tightly.

"Yes, dammit!" He took a deep breath and went on evenly, "When we first met, neither of us saw the other clearly. We were strangers who perhaps too quickly became lovers. Our mutual love of music and our passion held us together. We never looked for anything else."

Lacy felt her fingernails bite into her palms. "I told you, I don't think it's going to work," she said.

"Why not?" he demanded fiercely. "We can make it work! Think how wonderful it could be for us!"

"Damn you, don't you think I've thought of it?" she asked violently.

Suddenly he was in front of her chair, drawing her to her feet, his hands gripping her shoulders. "Let it out," he insisted softly. "Love me or hate me, but don't say you feel nothing! Don't look at me as if you feel nothing!"

She struggled for a brief moment to free herself but stopped when it proved a vain effort. The fight went out of her as suddenly as it had erupted. Her eyes lifted slowly to meet his. "What do you want me to say, Randall?" she asked.

"Just say that we can start over. Begin again." Tawny eyes searched hers with an odd, desperate pleading.

She looked at him mutely.

His hands lifted to frame her face. "Do you know what I want? I want you to look at me, Lacy. I want you to see the man you were never able to see."

Lacy tried desperately to ignore the warmth of his hands. "What are you talking about?"

"What did you see when we met at that first interview, Lacy? Tell me!" When she only looked at him in baffled incomprehension, he released her and turned suddenly away. Just as abruptly, he wheeled to face her.

"Don't you know? Then I'll tell you. You saw Randall St. James, legend of the music world." There was no conceit in his voice, only a curious, ragged bitterness. "A star fell from the sky and dangled in front of you, and you were blinded by it."

Lacy sank down into the chair behind her, staring up at him and feeling the chill of shock.

Curtly, each word bitten off, he went on. "You looked

at me as if I were a god, Lacy, do you know that? And no man ever wanted to feel less like a god in a woman's eyes. I was so taken with you—with your spirit. I wanted to be a man for you, but I just couldn't explain that to you.

"I didn't think it was wise for us to jump right into an affair—you were too special for that—but once we were on tour, and the longer you were with me, the harder it became to wait. Your presence ignited me, and your touch was fire, and you didn't even realize it. So I hoped that if we became lovers, you'd see through the glitter. But your lover was a legend, not a man. And when you left me, I thought you'd gotten bored with that legend."

"No," she whispered, appalled by her lack of perception months before. She was stunned to realize that he was right, that she had never understood him or his world because she had never really tried. She'd never really seen beyond the glitz and the glitter and the constant inconveniences of it all.

"Yes!" he shot at her. "What else could I think? All hell broke loose, and then you were gone! I thought you were tired of what you thought I was. Or afraid. Were you always afraid, Lacy? Afraid to get to close to a star, lest you get burned?"

Lacy realized that she was biting a knuckle only when she felt the pain. She wanted to tell him to stop, but no sound could force itself past the lump in her throat.

"Well, look at me now, Lacy!" He spread his arms in a defenseless gesture, a hot fury in the golden eyes. "Look at the god with the feet of clay. Look at the tarnished star. Maybe now you can see beneath the glitter and the glamour."

He sank down onto the couch, leaning forward to

bury his face in his hands. "Maybe now you can see me," he rasped.

For a long moment Lacy remained frozen. And then something inside her crumbled, and she went to him. She sat down beside him and touched his shoulder with a hand that didn't fear to touch a fallen star.

He turned suddenly, burying his face in her lap, his arms going around her blindly. "I need you, Lacy," he told her thickly, his voice muffled. I need you to tell me that there *is* something beneath the glitter... someone..."

She held him silently, aching inside. One hand stroked his black hair, the other smoothed the taut muscles of his back and shoulders. She briefly wondered if she pitied him but instantly knew it wasn't pity that was moving her so powerfully. It was something else.

And he had let her see the sensitive soul men usually guarded so jealously, so fiercely. He'd let her see his fear of being less of a man than he should be. His fear of being all surface glitter with nothing beneath it.

She wished she could turn back the clock for him and right all the wrongs. But she couldn't. She could only try to make amends now, in the present. She could only learn to see the man behind a star's blinding glitter.

"Lacy?" His voice was hesitant; he didn't lift his head.

She felt suddenly calmer. "Have you eaten?" she asked him softly.

He released her slowly and sat up, leaning back and looking at her guardedly. "No." His face was white, strained.

"Neither have I." She reached out to smooth back a lock of his black hair. "Want to share an omelette?"

His smile was tentative. "Sure."

She got up and went into the kitchen, flipping on the

light and beginning to gather what she needed for the meal. A moment later she felt his eyes on her and knew that he had followed her into the room.

"Lacy?"

She set a carton of eggs down on the counter and turned to look at him.

"Lacy, what are you offering?"

She looked at him for a long moment. So much to make up for. "You wanted us to get to know each other. A second chance to really see each other."

"Yes," he breathed softly.

"Then that's what I'm offering. Until Friday, as we agreed." She smiled. "But we're going to take it slowly," she added meaningfully, knowing how easily they could once again be blinded by the incredible passion they stirred in each other.

"Thank you, Lacy."

"How are your salads?" she asked lightly.

"Adequate," he said wryly.

"Then we'll have an adequate salad with our omelettes. The stuff's in the refrigerator."

Randall slept in her guest bedroom that night.

Lacy remained at home on Wednesday, calling Andrew to tell him she needed a little time for herself. He sounded glad to hear it and said he was entirely willing for her to take as much time as she needed.

It was a strange day.

Both she and Randall were tentative, hesitant. Neither wanted to disturb the elusive harmony between them. They talked over breakfast, guardedly at first and then with something approaching ease.

Neither really wished to go out, so they remained at

Lacy's apartment. But even there, just as it had been while they'd briefly shared an apartment in San Francisco, there were intrusions.

First Jake called. "Lacy! Top of the morning, darlin'. Put Randall on."

"Why?" she asked flatly.

Undaunted, Jake responded cheerfully, *"Musical World* magazine wants an interview, that's why! Put him on, sweetie."

Lacy covered the mouthpiece and waved the phone at Randall. "Jake."

Randall came over to take the phone, looking at her with a hint of anxiety in his eyes. "I'm sorry, Lacy."

"Never mind." She sighed. "Just tell him I'm not his darlin' or his sweetie."

She wasn't as patient when the second call came through.

"Miss Hamilton?"

"Yes?"

"Excuse me, Miss Hamilton, but is Mr. St. James there?"

Lacy gritted her teeth. "Who are you, and how did you get this number?" she demanded angrily.

The man sounded startled. "I'm the stage director at the concert hall, Miss Hamilton. I got your number from Mr. St. James's manager. I'm sorry, but I need to talk to him."

Lacy gestured to Randall, and when he came to take the phone, she snapped, "Jake's got my number, and there's nothing I can do about that. But you call him and tell him he'd damned well better not give it to anyone else!"

Randall caught the phone and her hand. "Lacy, I'm

sorry. I'll tell Jake not to bother us anymore."

Lacy got a grip on herself but shook her head in despair. "Some things never change..."

Since she went into the kitchen at that moment to start lunch, Lacy didn't know what Randall told Jake, but whatever it was, Jake must have taken it to heart. There were no more interruptions.

During the afternoon they progressed along the tentative path of a new beginning. Mostly they talked. About likes and dislikes. Sports and politics. Family. All the things they'd never found the time to delve into months ago, when their passion was new and there were never enough opportunities between professional matters to really search beyond the surface of things.

"I know you have a younger brother and sister," she commented at one point. "Are they musical?"

"Not really. Both play piano, but neither one of them ever wanted to compete. What about your brothers? They're older than you, aren't they?"

"Uh-huh."

"Musical?"

"Not in the least. Neither are my parents."

"Really? Both of mine are."

"I'll bet they were teaching you to play before you were out of diapers."

He chuckled softly, the sound a welcome one to Lacy's ears. "Almost. I was banging on the keys, anyway."

"I'll also bet that you were a precocious brat," she said wryly.

"Please. Not a brat."

"Sure."

"I swear. I was a little angel."

"Uh-huh. And the sun's about to set in the east."

"Neat trick."

"I'll say. Are you any good at crossword puzzles?"

"A whiz. Why?"

"I haven't done the one from the Sunday *Times* yet."

"I'll put on my thinking cap."

"Do that. Let's see . . . one across . . ."

It was a very strange day. They were, as Randall had wished, starting over. Learning to become comfortable with one another. It wasn't easy for Lacy to forget the complications of his career, to treat him as an interesting man she wanted to get to know and not the man the world called a modern-day legend. And she didn't think it was easy for Randall, either.

After his vulnerability of the night before, he was decidedly guarded. If he still felt the bitterness that had made him accuse her of not being able to see past the glitter of his career, he didn't show it. But he was still somehow slightly aloof, in spite of pleasant smiles and easy conversation, and she wondered for the first time just how badly her lack of perception had hurt him.

And it was very difficult to strive for lightness and humor when thoughts like that tortured her.

"Will you put that knitting down and pick up your cards?" he requested politely midway through the afternoon.

"Sorry." Lacy put her soon-to-be-scarf aside and picked up the cards lying face down on the coffee table. "It's just that you were taking so much time to decide whether or not to fold," she explained, arranging herself a bit more comfortably on the floor and leaning back against the couch to look across the table at him. He looked unbearably handsome, and she had to forcibly banish the impulse to reach out and touch him.

"Nonsense. I was just planning how much of my money to get back."

She looked at the pile of her winnings. "You have lost a tidy sum," she said gently.

"Don't rub it in." He tossed a dollar into the pot. Lacy matched his bid and raised him five dollars. He frowned at her, then tapped the tops of his cards thoughtfully.

She took a deep but silent breath and said quietly, "Randall, I didn't try to be blind."

He looked up, startled. Something flared deep in his eyes and then was hidden. He laid his cards down and gazed across at her. "I know that, Lacy."

"But you blame me for it," she insisted.

His jaw tightened slightly. "I can't help that."

"Why?" she whispered, the sudden stillness of the room creeping into her and clutching at her heart.

"I wanted you to be different." He was looking down, his fingers toying almost nervously with his cards. "I wanted you to see what was there. It never mattered that no one else saw. But you mattered."

"Randall—"

"You say that you hated my world," he interrupted. "But you never stopped to wonder how *I* felt about it. The ironic part is that I never stopped to wonder either— until you came along. But I'm wondering now."

She leaned toward him. "Randall, it's hard *not* to be blinded by the glitter surrounding you, because it's an ever-present thing. You can't escape from who and what you are. And I can't escape either."

"But I'm a *man* first," he said emphatically, almost as if he were trying to convince himself.

"To you and me, yes." She stared at him. "But not to the rest of the world. To them, you're a legend first and a man second."

He lifted glittering eyes to hers. "And legends aren't allowed to love, I suppose. But this one did. I loved you, you know."

She swallowed hard, feeling her heart pounding. "No . . . no, I was never sure of that. You never told me, you know."

"Would you have believed me if I had?" he asked bleakly.

She didn't answer, because she knew she probably wouldn't have believed him. Stars and gods didn't tie themselves to mortal women, after all.

"There's something I have to know Lacy."

"What is it?"

"Has there been anyone since me?"

Lacy looked down at her cards. The truth—that she'd been unable to even contemplate a relationship with another man, despite her irrepressibly romantic roommate's efforts—could be a weapon in his hands, but she couldn't lie. "No." She picked up her cards. "Bet or fold?" she asked evenly.

Silently he covered her bet.

She laid her cards down. A flush, in spades.

Randall laid down a royal flush. In hearts.

CHAPTER
Four

LACY WENT BACK to the office on Thursday, and Randall returned to the concert hall and his practicing. She knew they couldn't permit the mistake of leaping forward when they should walk slowly, and the tension between them had proven to her that they had to take this week together one step at a time.

Randall hadn't slept in her apartment.

And Lacy felt as though she were on a seesaw. Although determined to face the conflict between them, she had inexplicably shied away nervously upon discovering that the star she had loved had truly loved her.

What did he feel now? Lacy wasn't sure. He'd said that he needed her, and she believed that. But she still wasn't quite certain *why* he needed her—unless he was worried about possibly losing his musical gifts. And that was ironic! He needed her help because of the very gifts that had locked him away in his own world and built a wall between them!

But one thing was definite. If she and Randall were to have any sort of relationship, the guardedness and tension had to be conquered. Lacy had stopped silently denying that she wanted a relationship with him. She didn't try to explore her motives; there was something inside of her that was waiting, waiting for . . . what? She didn't know.

Randall came to her apartment after she got home from work, bearing with him steaks and wine and wearing a somewhat wary look. They shared the cooking chores in Lacy's tiny kitchen, getting in each other's way and being very polite about it. Finally Lacy's temper combined with her sense of humor, and she decided that enough was enough.

She halted in the center of the cramped floor space, arms crossed over her breasts and a wooden spoon tapping against her shoulder. She felt militant and probably looked it.

Randall turned, nearly collided with her, and carefully set the salad bowl he'd been carrying down onto the counter. He looked at her with a questioning lift of one eyebrow. "Something wrong?"

"Neither one of us is made of glass."

The other eyebrow rose. "That's wrong?"

She tapped the middle of his chest with her spoon. "See? You didn't break." She tapped her shoulder with the spoon again. "I didn't break, either. I think that proves we aren't made of glass."

"Looks that way," he agreed gravely.

"So tell me, why are we circling about each other as if we *were* made of glass?"

He stared down at her for a long moment, saying finally, "You could be opening up Pandora's box here, you realize."

"Maybe I like trouble," she said lightly.

"There'd better not be any 'maybe' about it."

"We're adults, Randall."

"That's true."

"With self-control."

"Uh-huh." He leaned back against the counter.

"Restraint."

"Certainly."

"Disinterest in a physical relationship."

Randall appeared to think that one over.

"You agreed that we needed to start over and go slowly," she reminded him.

"Did I?" he asked blandly.

"Yes." She glared at him.

"Must have been out of my mind at the time."

Lacy blinked and tried not to giggle. He sounded so rueful. "Maybe we'd better define this relationship of ours," she suggested.

"If you insist. Although I think we should just let it develop naturally. You know, no limits and no boundaries," he said slowly.

She ignored that. "We have to be friends first. And friends," she said firmly, "aren't afraid of bumping into each other occasionally. They touch casually." She thought about that for a moment, then repeated, "Casually."

Randall hesitated, then said very neutrally, "Friends are also honest with one another. I don't think I can touch you casually . . . friend."

Lacy wished suddenly that she hadn't tampered with the lock on Pandora's box. At the same time, she was very weary of the no-man's land between them. There had to be, she thought, some middle ground. And she'd gone this far, after all.

"Randall, I don't want to make the same mistake I made before. I don't want to find myself in an affair with a man I don't know. But this . . . whatever it is . . . between us—I don't want that either. There are too many things we're afraid to say, too many things we're afraid to do. What kind of basis is that to build on?" She hesitated, then added painfully, "I don't want to be afraid of you again, Randall."

He reached out abruptly and pulled her to him, still leaning back against the counter as he held her. He rubbed his chin against the top of her head. "I don't want you to be afraid of me either," he muttered bitterly. When he went on, his voice was calm again and unexpectedly gentle. "All right, friend. I'll try to be the gentleman you once accused me of not being." She stirred uneasily, and his arms tightened slightly around her. "I won't do anything to mess things up between us, Lacy. I promise you that."

Lacy felt the gentle touch of his hands on her back, and she felt his heart thudding quickly against her. She could feel the desire in him, the tension of muscles held under strict control, the throbbing of need he couldn't hide. A man's need, not a legend's. She was awed to realize that such simple touching could do that to him.

A part of her wanted to tell him to never mind being a gentleman, dammit. But that other part of her was still waiting, and she still didn't know for what. And until she did...

Randall was setting her away from him, gently but firmly. There was a faint white line of tension around his smiling mouth. "Hey, friend, the steaks are burning."

They weren't, but Lacy got the point.

By Friday evening Lacy was on edge. It hadn't helped that she'd been bombarded with calls all day at work as well as at home; although Jake swore he wasn't responsible, the press had discovered where and with whom Randall St. James had been spending a great deal of his time lately.

And the calls had started at 7:00 A.M. First had been a sly society reporter asking arch questions about "rekindled" romances. Following her had been others. Lacy had even gotten a call at work from a magazine asking her—ironically—to give them an interview about "the man behind the legend." Lacy marvelled at the speed at which information spread in Randall's world, and she frantically held on to her composure while refusing comment.

Now she stood in the wings and gazed out over the stage, seeing the other musicians tuning their instruments, seeing the grand piano standing in lonely splendor, hearing the muffled chatter of the audience. The concert would begin shortly.

She half turned to watch Randall as he paced restlessly. He was shatteringly handsome in his black tails, his face set in pre-concert concentration.

The lights out front dimmed; the screechy clash of instruments faded into silence. Randall came over to where Lacy was standing, a strangely blind look in his darkened tawny eyes as he gazed out at the stage. His hand lifted almost absently to stroke up and down her spine through the thin silk of her ivory dress, as though he needed the touch of something warm and alive beneath his gifted fingers.

"You're tense," he murmured.

She felt a tremor in his long, limber fingers, but she knew that it was the music this time, not her. "So are you. Randall..." She looked at him mutely, wanting to wish him luck but afraid to betray her sudden awareness that the concert wouldn't go well. He was too tense, too keyed up to perform well, and she knew it. And he still looked so tired.

He gazed directly at her then. "I'm afraid, Lacy," he said bluntly. "For the first time in my life, I don't want to go out there."

Instinctively, she reached out for his free hand, finding it reaching out for hers. Both their hands were cold, she realized. What could she say? "They're waiting for you, Randall." Almost immediately she silently cursed herself for the hopelessly inadequate words. How could she help him when she didn't know *how?*

But it must have been enough. Enough, anyway, for the Randall St. James who'd always been a consummate professional, who would never think to disappoint an audience with a no-show.

Squeezing her hand almost convulsively, he bent his head to kiss her briefly, and then he was gone. Lips throbbing, Lacy stared after him. She was vividly aware of the audience applauding, of the spotlight on Randall like the merciless eye it was. It was Lacy who winced at the cruel eye, knowing it would let nothing be hidden.

She listened as the music started, listened with every sense straining.

Hers were trained senses. The larger part of the audience, she knew, would notice nothing amiss. And there was certainly no discordant clash of notes, no vital mistake of Randall's making.

But it was wrong. All wrong. There were almost imperceptible hesitations, minute pauses that had nothing to do with interpretation, whole passages rushed, others dragged out.

At first Randall played adequately—technically with near-brilliant precision, emotionally as though he were a puppet. Then, slowly, technique deserted him, and emotion rushed in to fill the void. Destructive emotion.

It was worse than Lacy had expected.

Her throat went dry, and her heart pounded with dull agony. She wanted to draw the curtain between the audience and the man punishing himself on the stage. She knew that the critics, at least, heard what she heard: the pain and frustrated rage of a musician who was no longer in control of his music.

And she hurt desperately for him.

She endured the remainder of the concert, the image in her mind one of a strong king suddenly faltering before his subjects. The subjects applauded, and the king—his pallor unnoticed in the white-washing glare of the spotlight—took his bows. Then he moved purposefully toward the wings.

Lacy picked up her jacket from a nearby stool and shrugged into it automatically. There would be, she knew, no encores; she didn't have to see the erratic pulsing in Randall's temple or his blazing eyes to know that.

He caught her arm in a tight grip and steered her toward the stage door. "Let's get the hell out of here," he muttered.

Like a robot, Lacy accompanied him. Outwardly she

was calm. But inwardly the wild ferocity of her emotions was painful. In a single blinding instant as Randall had bowed before the audience, she'd realized what she had been waiting for. It had been this, this performance, this proof that Randall had not lied about something being wrong.

And Lacy was suddenly shamefully aware now of why she had waited for this night. A part of her was glad. Randall truly did need her now; she'd never again have to share him with the world, which would callously shun a worn-out legend.

If, that is, she didn't help him to find what he'd lost . . .

Flashbulbs caught them in blinding lights as they emerged from the stage door and out into the crowd of fans and reporters. Strident questions from the press were, to Lacy, mercifully unintelligible.

Except for one.

"Mr. St. James, what went wrong tonight?"

Randall ignored the question. And for the first time in his career, Randall also ignored the autograph books and programs held out for his signature. The stage guards provided a flying wedge for them to hurry through the crowd, and within minutes they were in the limousine.

In darkness and tense silence Lacy stared straight ahead and determinedly filed her own emotions away in the back of her mind. She'd sort them out later.

"Randall?" She turned her head to see his flawless profile illuminated by the lights of passing cars and bright nightspots. His features were so set that his face might have been carved from marble. "I'm . . . sorry, Randall."

He reached out to find her hand in the darkness, his own now almost feverishly hot. "Not now, Lacy," he said huskily. "I don't want to talk about it now."

Her fingers twined with his, and she held his hand tightly.

After weaving its way through the heavy Friday-night traffic, the limousine finally pulled up to the curb outside Lacy's apartment building. As if in unspoken understanding, the driver remained where he was as Randall got out and helped Lacy out. He was still holding her hand.

Before he could speak, she did. "Send the car away, Randall. Stay here tonight." She decided he could take that invitation any way he liked.

Randall stood looking down at her for a long moment. In a hard voice he finally said, "I don't want your pity, Lacy."

She didn't flinch. She simply continued to gaze up at him. "You know what your hotel will be like, Randall. Press, phone calls, all the rest. At least here you'll have a better chance at peace and quiet."

He seemed to consider briefly; then he nodded and bent to speak with the driver. The long black car slid away from the curb, and they silently walked up the steps. Inside her apartment, Randall went immediately to the living room window and stared out. He was withdrawn, somewhere else.

Lacy watched him for a minute or so. She knew he still wasn't ready to talk about what had happened. An open wound was a painful thing, and he wasn't ready to share that pain with her. But it hurt her. She went into her bedroom, leaving him alone.

She took a shower and donned the black caftan. Wryly, she considered that choice. Black. Mourning. Shaking off the thought, she returned to the living room. Randall was at the window again, but he'd shed his coat and tie, and his customarily proud stance was obscured by hunched shoulders. He was still withdrawn.

She couldn't stand it. "Randall, I want to help you. Tell me how to help you."

He stirred slightly. Without turning to face her, he said flatly, "You can't help me, Lacy. You still can't even see me."

"I'm trying." She took a step toward him. "But to-night—tonight you won't *let* me see you."

Randall began to pace jerkily, his movements uncontrolled, as though he had to keep moving or he'd jump out of his skin. "No, not tonight. Tonight I don't want you to see me. I don't want your pity."

"It isn't pity!" She took a deep breath, trying to weave together the tangled skeins of her thoughts. And she was suddenly angry. "Dammit, Randall, you can't have it both ways!" Her outburst brought him around to face her, obviously surprised. She rushed on. "You can't pick and choose the moments when you allow me to see you. You can't shut me out and expect me to get to know you.

"It's what I was talking about before: There are too many things we can't say. It's not just the past, don't you see? You get to know someone by building a—a composite picture of the bad times as well as the good. How can I know you if you shut me out during the bad times?"

"Do you want to see me on my knees, Lacy?" he asked harshly. "Is that what you want to see?"

"I want to see what's there! I *have* to see what's there, or it's no good!" She glared at him, deliberately and fiercely digging for the truth. "What are you feeling, Randall? What are you feeling right now, this moment? Tell me!"

"Alone!" he rapped out suddenly, his voice rough, ragged. "I feel alone." Tension visibly drained from him; the fire had gone from his golden eyes, leaving them dark and bleak.

Lacy went to him, placing a hand on his chest. Softly she said, "You're not alone, Randall. Not unless you want to be."

He looked at her, looked long and hard, as though wondering if her words were motivated by pity, her gesture by sympathy. Whatever he saw in her eyes must have reassured him; a faint glow kindled to life somewhere in the depths of his own.

Very quietly Lacy said, "Was it all my fault, Randall—that I didn't see you? Or was it partly yours? Did you hide behind the glitter, where no one could see you?"

He reached up to touch her face lightly, his eyes following the movement as his long fingers traced the curve of her cheek, the line of her jaw. "It never mattered that no one saw," he said a second time. "Until you. Then it mattered."

"And then?" She was gently persistent; she felt it was important that no guilt remain between them, that each accepted a part of the fault. "How long had you hidden by then? Years? Did you help strip away the glitter so that I could see you? Or did you expect me to strip it away all by myself?"

His free hand lifted and joined the other in framing her face, and a soft, rough sigh escaped him. "You're right," he admitted. "I expected you to see something I wasn't able to show. I haven't been very fair, have I, Lacy?"

She shook her head slightly, denying his words. "It's not that. We always see from our own perspective, don't we? You just didn't realize how thoroughly you'd hidden yourself—any more than I realized there was more to you than what I saw."

"We can do better now," he said, half hope and half promise.

"We can do better now." Lacy smiled. "Beginning with tonight. Tell me what happened tonight, Randall."

He grimaced, but there was a glint of humor in his eyes. "You're going to pull me through this in spite of myself, aren't you, honey?"

The endearment startled Lacy, but it warmed her as well. She didn't stop to wonder why. "Somebody has to," she told him with mock gravity.

He bent his head to kiss the tip of her nose, and then he was leading her toward the couch. He sat her down in one corner and then rather deliberately sat down about a foot away from her. Lacy didn't have to ask why he'd chosen to put distance between them; she knew. She half turned to face him, waiting patiently.

Resting his arm along the back of the couch between them, Randall looked at her steadily. "What happened tonight, eh? I thought it was obvious what happened tonight. I blew it."

"Why?" she asked simply.

"That's like asking how many angels can dance on the head of a pin." Then he sighed softly, seemingly more analytical now, more able to view his performance objectively. "I lost my concentration. First there was no feeling for the music, and then there was too much—all of it wrong. I don't *know* what happened, Lacy. I just know that the same thing's been happening a lot lately."

"When was the last time you had a vacation? I mean a real vacation, with no piano within reach?"

Randall shook his head. "I don't know. Years, I suppose."

Lacy was suddenly impatient. And then the impatience faded, to be replaced by near anger. Anger at him. Anger at the music that had so obsessed him for so long. "Do you have any hobbies, any interests other than music?" The question was sharp, rapped out.

He looked at her curiously. "You're angry," he murmured, ignoring the question. "At me?"

"At you," she confirmed evenly. "Randall, don't you see what you've done? When did you begin playing the piano? At the age of five. So, for twenty years you worked to be the best. Hours every day. *Every day.* And when you were twenty-five, there wasn't a critic in the world who wouldn't have agreed that you were brilliant, that you were the best. A legend in your own time."

Randall stirred impatiently. "Lacy—"

"Listen to me!" She glared at him. "That was ten years ago, Randall. What have you been doing since then? Where do you go from perfection? How can you climb higher when you're at the very top?"

"I wasn't perfect," he told her roughly.

"No." Her voice was very quiet. "You weren't perfect. The world thought you were, but you didn't agree. So you kept pushing yourself. I think that's when you stopped controlling the music, Randall, and when it started controlling you."

His long, gifted fingers drummed rhythmically against the back of the couch. "Armchair analysis?" he asked with terse sarcasm.

She looked at him steadily. "Do you know how the dictionary defines obsession, Randall? As 'an abnormal preoccupation with a persistent idea or desire.'" She smiled mirthlessly. "I looked it up."

Randall was frowning. "You're wrong, Lacy. My music is an extension of myself. A form of self-expression."

"It *was*. Once. When you played because you loved the sound of it, because you wanted to play. To be the best was a natural ambition. And ambition took you to the top, but it couldn't take you any further. Don't you see?" She stared at him, willing him to understand. "With ambition, you control the music; with obsession, it controls you."

There was a curiously blank look in Randall's eyes. "You're saying that . . . I turned into the slave instead of the master."

"Yes!"

"And so?" He was watching her, a strange intensity now lighting his eyes. "Are you telling me I should give up my music?"

She leaned forward, unthinkingly placing a hand over the one resting on his thigh. "No, of course not. Randall, your music will be a part of you all the days of your life. But you shouldn't exist for it. It exists for *you*. Without you, music is nothing more than random squiggles on a sheet of paper. A piano is nothing more than a man-made instrument, silent until you touch it."

"Or until you do," he murmured.

"No. I play the piano, but you make *music*."

Randall was shaking his head slowly, his eyes locked with hers, and Lacy felt frustrated at her inability to make herself clear. Then, as he spoke, she realized that she *had* made herself clear.

"Did you hide thoughts like that from me before?" he asked huskily.

Lacy shook her head, silently acknowledging how removed they really had been from each other. "No, I simply didn't think those thoughts before. But . . . I think I'm right."

His hand slid from beneath hers and then immediately covered it, so she could feel the warmth and the hard strength of his thigh. "I think that perhaps you are. At least partly."

Lacy suddenly realized that she was on her knees on the couch—and far closer to him than she'd meant to be. But she couldn't pull away. His golden eyes held her spellbound; she watched in utter fascination as they darkened to honey, their liquid depths sweetly calling her. A siren song, she thought vaguely. But there was no mast to lash herself to.

"Randall . . . it's too soon . . ." she murmured, as though he'd spoken aloud.

"I know." His voice was a mere breath of sound, husky, impeded. "I know. Just let me hold you for a little while. Please, honey . . ." His free hand lifted from the back of the couch, reaching to curve warmly around the nape of her neck. He pulled her toward him slowly, as if afraid she'd withdraw at the first sign of haste.

But Lacy didn't withdraw. She obeyed the gentle, insistent command of his hand, leaning forward slowly as he leaned back. Her hand on his thigh shifted to his chest, and she felt the hardness of his hips against her stomach as he lay fully back on the couch. His arms moved slowly to enfold her.

Lacy stared into honey eyes, feeling a tug at something deep inside her, a tug that was painful and yet sweet. She reached out to touch his face, to trace the handsome features with the sensitive touch of one who saw through the fingers.

She was dimly aware that they had never shared a moment such as this, a moment of gentleness and closeness with unspoken yet understood desire throbbing between them. A moment out of time, to be cherished, to be grasped at desperately because it was so rare.

And Randall seemed to feel it as well. He made no attempt to kiss her or touch her with demand. He simply held her, as if that satisfied some deep, starving need within him. Held her and gazed quietly into her eyes.

It was a long time before either of them spoke, and when Randall finally did, his voice was hushed. "You've been very patient with all the interruptions this week. But I think you and I need some time alone together. Really alone. My family has a vacation cabin up in Maine. Do you think your office could spare you for a couple of weeks? My tour is over, and I'll tell Jake that I'm going to disappear—and that if he values his job, he won't look for me. How about it?"

Not even hesitating, she nodded silently. She was overdue for a vacation anyway, and Andrew wouldn't mind.

"I'm glad." His mouth quirked slightly. "You said something about outside interests before. You were trying to show me how narrow my life is, weren't you?"

Again she nodded.

"And so?"

"And so." She smiled. "Perhaps I can show you how to look at life as if you were tone-deaf."

Randall reached to stroke her hair, then used gentle pressure to guide her until her cheek was resting comfortably against his chest. She could no longer gaze into his golden eyes, but his hand continued to softly stroke her hair, and his deep voice was indescribably soothing.

"Perhaps you can. I think I'd like to learn from you, Lacy. And you've always known, haven't you? How to look at life as if you were tone-deaf, I mean. You've always been able to play at life."

Lacy allowed her eyes to drift closed. "My parents taught me that," she murmured. "You wouldn't think a career Air Force man would have a sense of humor, but Dad does. And Mom wouldn't be Mom if she didn't do ridiculous things like invite the general's wife for lunch and then open the door wearing jeans and demand help with the cooking."

Randall chuckled softly. "I'd like to meet them."

"Mmmm." The tensions of the past week had taken their toll, and Lacy felt her eyes involuntarily closing. "They'd like you," she mumbled drowsily. She was faintly aware of his voice asking softly, "Would they?" It was her last coherent moment before she drifted into sleep.

She heard music in her dreams, beautiful music. There was a king sitting before the piano, bathed in golden light, and Lacy watched and listened, enthralled. Then silence descended, smothering the music, although the king's long fingers continued to move over the keys. Frowning, her heart thudding heavily, Lacy saw the king's glittering crown begin to topple. In slow motion, its golden light reflecting off oddly dim jewels, the crown tumbled to the floor and rolled to Lacy's feet. She bent slowly and picked it up. Her fingers rubbed the cloudy jewels until they were bright again, and she looked toward the piano. The king had stopped playing his weirdly silent song and had turned on the bench, staring at her with a proud, quiet dignity. She wanted to walk to him, to take the crown back to him. But she stood rooted in place, unable to move.

It's just a dream, she tried to tell herself. Just a dream. But still he stared at her. She fingered the crown in her hands, remembering the music. If she brought his crown back to him, the music would begin again, she knew. The music was beautiful... but it hurt her. It hurt her, and it took something away from her. Slowly, with great, painful effort, Lacy turned away from him. Away from the golden eyes and the silent, despairing plea. She walked into the darkness of the wings, feeling the sharp edges of the crown bite into her fingers, feeling the wetness of tears on her cheeks...

The darkness seemed to close around her. It was warm and comforting and curiously solid, brushing the tears from her cheeks and prying her fingers from the crown. A voice reached out to her in the darkness, soft, anxious. But Lacy was ashamed, and she didn't answer. Selfish! She was selfish, and she didn't deserve the concern in the worried voice. But the voice cradled her in gentleness, and she could feel herself floating away with it.

Softness cushioned her after a time, and she clung with sudden desperation to something warm and strong. She heard her voice pleading helplessly and barely recognized it as her own. And then she heard his voice, the king's, the king she had cruelly walked away from. He was swearing softly, but he stayed with her. He was kinder than she had been, and he didn't leave her alone...

The bell ringing scant inches away finally awakened Lacy, but she didn't open her eyes or move. Hazy images presented themselves to her mind until finally the correct one emerged. The telephone. The phone was ringing. It had to be the phone, because she never set her alarm clock. She listened. Yes, it was the phone. Alexander Graham Bell, she decided with sleepy mutiny, should have been strangled at birth.

She felt movement and frowned. Had she moved? No, she didn't think she had. She was too warm and comfortable to move. And then she heard a voice, and all thoughts of sleep left her.

"You have terrible timing, Jake. I'll talk to you later. Don't call again."

Lacy's eyes snapped open. First she saw the phone cord trailing across her chest. She followed the cord to the receiver, which in turn was being held by a masculine hand. Unusually foggy, Lacy considered these salient points. Phone. Cord. Man. *Man?*

Randall reached over her to replace the receiver. "Good morning," he murmured.

She shifted her eyes far enough to stare at him. They were in bed. *Her* bed. Under the covers. She was afraid to lift the blanket and find out what she was wearing— or what she wasn't wearing. *He* was obviously wearing nothing from the waist up.

"How did this happen?" she squeaked.

"You mean, why are we in bed together?" Randall clarified bluntly. "Well, you fell asleep on the couch, and I carried you in here. And since you didn't want me to leave you, I didn't."

The vision of herself clinging like a limpet to Randall brought the blood rushing to Lacy's face. But Randall was smiling with curiously gentle whimsy. He ran a finger down her flushed cheek.

"You must have been having a nightmare," he explained. "You were crying in your sleep, and your hands were clenched together so tightly that your fingernails were cutting into your skin. As if you were holding something and afraid to lose it. So I carried you here and stayed with you."

With astonishing clarity, Lacy's dream flooded her conscious mind. She swallowed hard. "I—thank you," she got out haltingly. Then she remembered the soft, swearing voice. And her thoughts must have been reflected on her face, for Randall's smile widened.

"I won't say that I expected to sleep. The thought of holding you in my arms all night and being a gentleman about it didn't exactly thrill me. Strangely enough, though, I did sleep." Laughter lit his eyes. "Just don't ask me to do it too often, honey. I'm not made of stone."

Lacy wanted to respond to his amusement, wanted to treat the whole thing lightly. But sensual memories triggered by waking up beside him rushed into her mind. The one thing that had always been perfect between them was their lovemaking. Without those precious hours, Lacy knew she would have lost patience with the demands of his career long before she had.

The memories tortured her now, brushing her nerve endings with fire and setting her heart to pounding. She knew that she had to leave his side, had to get out of the bed before she lost her common sense and provoked a leap their tenuous relationship wasn't yet ready for.

But it was too late. She could see that in his eyes, could see the disappearance of amusement and the flare of awareness. And she knew what would happen even before he caught his breath and leaned toward her, even before she felt the fierce demand of his kiss.

Her arms lifted to encircle his neck, and she saw that she was still wearing her caftan. There was no relief in the thought, as there would have been only moments earlier. There was only annoyance. Her clothing was a barrier, and she didn't want any barriers between them now.

"Lacy," he whispered raggedly when his lips left hers to feather hotly down her throat. "Honey, I know it's too soon, but I need you so badly! Don't tell me to stop."

She had no intention of telling him to stop. He'd been right—nothing mattered but this. Not now. She tilted her chin up instinctively to allow more scope for his explorations, not even offering token resistance when his fingers found the fastenings of her caftan and began to free her of the garment. She helped him toss it aside and waited impatiently while he coped with his trousers.

And then she lost herself in the wonder of his touch, lost herself in the wild storm of passion he unleashed. She gasped when his mouth captured a throbbing nipple, her fingers tangling in his hair and then sliding down to mold the rippling muscles of his shoulders and back.

She could feel the hungry caresses of his hands in every fiber, every nerve of her body. The empty ache inside of her grew, tension gripping her and building with astonishing speed. Her restless movements were uncontrollable, and the need in her flooded her with molten fire.

"Randall," she pleaded, hardly aware of speaking, aware only of the crucial need to end the sweetly painful tension.

"Darling," he murmured hoarsely, rising above her and gazing down at her, his eyes darkly glowing.

Lacy held him fiercely, welcomed him eagerly. In knowledge and instinct, she moved with him, inciting them both to an exploding release more shattering than they had ever experienced before. She cried out breathlessly at the soaring peak, hearing him groan out her name raggedly, and feeling truly at peace for the first time in months.

CHAPTER
Five

WHEN LACY SLIPPED from the bed a long time later, Randall was asleep. She realized again how weary he was and knew that she would have accompanied him to Maine for no other reason than to see that he got some rest. But she had other reasons, of course.

She took a quick shower, donned a pair of jeans and a sweater, and headed for the kitchen to make breakfast, her sock-clad feet making no noise. She didn't let herself think too much, but one thought refused to be denied.

Their relationship had taken a leap it wasn't ready for, and she knew it.

She began to prepare breakfast, her motions automatic. She listened to the radio but didn't really hear the music. She wondered if Randall clearly realized that they couldn't allow a physical relationship to obscure the problems between them. Would he understand?

Lacy sighed ruefully. Did she understand herself?

Warm lips nuzzled the back of her neck.

She turned quickly and looked up at him, and something of her feelings must have shown on her face, because his smile died slowly.

"Randall, it didn't change things," she whispered.

His beautiful hands lifted to frame her face warmly, and his beautiful eyes probed. Then he sighed. "I was afraid you'd say that."

She reached up to grasp his wrists, feeling the tiny twin pulses. "It was too soon—we both know that."

"Do you regret it?" he asked.

Her fingers tightened around his wrists. "No. But, Randall, we can't let passion overshadow everything else. And it will, if we let it. I want to be very sure this time. I want it to work."

After a moment, Randall nodded and smiled. "That's good enough for me. At least now you aren't fighting me." He bent his head to kiss her quickly. "But I hope you realize it won't be easy."

Lacy found herself smiling. "I think we'll cope. Now, if you'd like to go and shave while I finish breakfast? Then I'll call Andrew and tell him that his star translator needs a vacation. When are we off to Maine?"

"How about right after lunch?" he suggested, matching her light tone.

She lifted a brow and then nodded. "Sounds fine to me."

They were both packed by lunchtime, and after sharing a light meal at Lacy's apartment, they were on their way to Maine. Randall had rented a car, saying that driving relaxed him, and so they fought the city traffic, left it behind them, and headed north.

Lacy was somewhat subdued, confusion and a disquieting sense of conflict suddenly roiling within her. She knew herself well enough to know that, once involved with Randall again, she'd end up being jealous of the entire world. And that, she realized with a sense of shame, explained why part of her felt almost relieved at the knowledge that something was wrong with Randall's music. If he lost his music, she would lose what she knew in her heart was her rival.

But she also knew what the loss of his music would do to Randall, and she simply couldn't wish that pain on him. So the compassion within her was warring with her woman's desire to eliminate a rival. If she somehow managed to help Randall find his music, she would be strengthening the wall between them. If she didn't help him, she would be helping to destroy her rival—and possibly Randall as well.

Either way, she'd lose.

She wondered dimly when she had realized that she still loved Randall. At the concert? No, even before, she decided. That first night, when she had gone to dinner with him because she'd been worried about him. A part of her had known then.

A part of her had known throughout those lonely months since she'd left him, she silently admitted.

Randall had shown himself to be more than willing to rebuild a stronger relationship between them. And Lacy? She now knew she wanted that as well. More than anything in the world.

She'd have to find her way out of this dilemma. She'd have to find a way to help Randall and still keep her fears at bay.

Once they were clear of the city and well on their way, Randall seemed to notice her quietness.

"Regrets?" he asked.

She looked over at him, at his beautiful face, and knew that, despite her confusion, she had no regrets about this trip. "No," she answered honestly.

"Then what's the matter?" He sent a sidelong glance at her. "You haven't said ten words since we started out." He reached over to clasp her hand.

"Nothing." She smiled at him, pushing her worries aside. And after another probing glance at her, Randall allowed the subject to drop.

They were silent for a long time, content to listen to the soft classical music on the radio, their hands bonding them together across the gear console.

Absently, Lacy watched the beautiful landscape of Massachusetts slip past them, to be replaced gradually by the rolling hills of New Hampshire.

"There's a summer haven here, isn't there?" she asked suddenly.

Randall nodded. "For writers, artists. Composers."

"Have you been there?"

He hesitated, then said, "Last summer."

"Really?" She abandoned the scenic view to look at him. "You always told me you didn't know enough about music to compose."

"I don't." He smiled crookedly. "But I'm trying."

Lightly she said, "Maybe you'll let me hear some of your compositions. I'm sure there's a piano at your family's cabin."

"Yes, there's a piano." His voice had flattened suddenly.

Lacy looked at him, wondering if he were brooding about the botched concert. Before she could ask, he'd changed the subject.

"Tell me, how did you wind up being a translator? I've always wondered."

She accepted the change of subject. "I was told in college that I was a 'natural' linquist. I'd never thought about it until then, but I suppose growing up in several different countries gave me an unusual opportunity."

He glanced at her, amusement in his eyes. "Is that why you occasionally sound about as American as Britain's queen?"

She smiled. "I think that usually happens to Americans who spend years abroad. And I didn't really live here until I started college. My father was transferred out of the States when I was six months old. Kids pick up languages more easily than adults; I got about half a dozen languages and quite a few dialects in seventeen years. My instructors in college told me that my ear for music was a definite advantage, and then they worked busily to smooth out my grammar."

Randall laughed. "Which brings us back to the original question. How did you wind up being a translator?"

"Oh, it seemed the thing to do. Languages always fascinated me, and apititude tests kept prodding me in that direction. I applied to Andrew's West Coast office in San Francisco. When he flew in for a visit a few months ago, he asked me to transfer to New York." She didn't mention that she'd jumped at the chance to get away from San Francisco and its reminders of her four months with Randall. "I've been there ever since, barring the time spent abroad on assignment."

"And you enjoy the work?"

"Very much. It has its trying moments, though—or days as the case may be." She laughed. "I had to shepherd a dozen teenage girls across Greece a couple of months ago. That was fun. Their teacher was as fascinated as they were by dark-eyed fishermen, and I had the devil of a time keeping them all out of trouble. It cost Andrew one hell of a bonus when I came home."

"I'll bet." Randall grinned at her. "And you were never tempted by any of those dark-eyed fishermen, huh?"

"Never," she said lightly. Obsidian couldn't compare with gold—but she didn't tell him that.

"The fishermen's loss."

Lacy decided to change the subject. "Where, exactly, are we going in Maine?"

"By the way," Randall murmured teasingly.

She shot him a mock glare. "Answer the question, friend. If you don't, I'll start thinking you're taking me up here to sell me into white slavery."

"I'd never sell you," he said calmly.

Lacy let that pass. "Where are we going?"

"North of Portsmouth, south of Portland. The cabin is right on the coast."

"Really? I've never been in that part of the state."

"I didn't know you'd been in Maine at all," he commented.

"Uh-huh. Visited the parents one summer while I was in college. Daddy was stationed at Loring at the time."

"That's up near Canada, isn't it?"

"Just a few miles from the border."

He glanced at her curiously. "Where are your parents now?"

"Still at Holloman, in New Mexico. They've been there nearly a year now."

"Will they stay there much longer?"

"Nope. I hear it'll be Brooks next. That's in San Antonio, Texas."

Randall shook his head. "They don't stay in one place

long, do they? What happened to the overseas duty?"

"Dad requested stateside. He and Mom didn't care for being so far away from all of us."

"Your brothers live in the States, don't they?"

"Mmmm. Daniel lives in Seattle with his wife and two kids. He does something—I've never understood exactly what—with computers. Mark is newly married and living—stationed—in San Diego."

"Air Force?" Randall asked with a sidelong look.

"Nope. Navy." Lacy grinned. "Dad calls him a traitor whenever they meet." She listened to the pleasant sound of Randall's chuckle for a moment. "What about your family? Where are they?"

"My parents live in Boston. My brother Scott is married and living in Florida; like your brother, he does something with computers. Lynn is in college in Boston."

Lacy was surprised. "I didn't realize she was so young."

"Twenty-one."

"So you had to play big brother?"

"No," Randall said soberly. "Fourteen years is a big gap when you're kids. And then there was my music. No, Scott played big brother; he's four years older than Lynn. I . . . barely know them."

Lacy winced. She wondered if anyone had ever troubled to know the real Randall. A certified, bona fide child prodigy, she reflected, was a thing apart—alone. And a prodigy grown to genius was even more alone. She looked at Randall and ached inside. Had he ever been given the chance to mix with people outside the limelight? She didn't think so.

And that was the tragedy. The legend could never have overwhelmed the man if the man had been secure in himself. And being treated as a man rather than a legend would have helped to make him secure.

A genius was a gift to the world. But Lacy understood now why so many of them had died or burned out young. Even with a great gift as compensation, who could stand to be alone for so long?

"You're staring at me," he observed, both eyes on the road.

"Can you feel it?" she asked lightly.

"All the way down to my bones."

"I'll rent myself out as an X-ray machine, shall I?"

Randall shot her a look, a smile tugging at the corners of his mouth. "You sound cheerful all of a sudden."

He was right. Having come to one clear understanding about Randall's problem, she felt somehow lighter of heart. "I am cheerful. When do we arrive at the cabin?"

"In about half an hour."

"Wonderful. Do you want your hand back? I noticed that we barely made that last curve; perhaps you should put both hands on the wheel?"

Randall blinked and glanced over at her. This time his sidelong look lasted a little longer, and his eyes seemed to be probing her. "Something's happened," he said bemusedly. He kept peering over at her, giving his driving a bit less than rational attention. Lacy finally reached out and turned his chin, then placed his hand back on the wheel firmly.

"There's a car that just passed us," she said calmly, "whose driver has narrowly escaped death. I'm sure his whole life flashed in front of his eyes, and he'll stop at the next phone booth to call his wife and apologize for taking her for granted. Watch what you're doing, Randall."

Randall looked at the road. However, since the next two curves were taken at something less than a safe speed, he didn't seem to have his mind on driving. And he kept glancing at Lacy from the corner of his eye.

"We've finally put some obstacle behind us, haven't we?" he said.

"We've put something behind us. And if you don't slow down," she added cheerfully, "we'll never live to enjoy what's ahead of us!"

He blinked, apparently realized what he was doing, and immediately slowed the car. "I'm glad," he murmured. "I'm very glad, Lacy."

"So am I." Lacy smiled at him and turned her happy attention to the view she'd virtually ignored until then. Never mind the future, she decided. Let it take care of itself.

They'd turned off a major highway and onto a less traveled coastal road. The Atlantic stretched out to the east, green-gray and a little angry-looking. The sandy beaches were deserted, there was a brisk breeze, and lowering clouds were building steadily. A fit day for only the hardy, Lacy decided, but Nature was beautiful in her stormy mood.

"We're going to get rained on," she observed.

Randall glanced up at the clouds. "Not until tonight, I think."

The car turned into a driveway, high hedges providing privacy for the house they were approaching. The house was still hidden by the hedges when Randall stopped the car, but Lacy could see the roof.

And it wasn't exactly a cabin. Judging by the roof line, which sprawled in nearly every direction, the building could be comprised of around half a dozen bedrooms without skimping on other rooms.

Lacy sent Randall a speaking look. "A cabin?"

"A cabin of sorts." He grinned at her.

She sighed, then opened the door as Randall opened

his. Immediately they were hit by a blast of chill air—
and the blaring sound of rock music played at full vol-
ume.

Climbing from the car, Lacy shut her door and then
looked at Randall with the lift of an eyebrow. "Is your
homecoming always saluted like this?" she asked politely.

Randall stared at her across the car's low top. "There
shouldn't be anyone here," he said somewhat grimly.

Before Lacy could respond, an interruption presented
itself. It burst through the hedge nearly at Lacy's feet,
tongue lolling and bright brown eyes peering out of tangled brown fur.

A masculine voice from the other side of the hedge
howled, "Sam! Come back here, you mutt!" in an interesting tenor.

Instinctively, Lacy bent quickly and scooped up the
little dog, holding his happily quivering body in one arm.
A friendly creature, the dog washed her chin with an
impossibly long tongue.

Next through the hedge was Sam's human twin, making his own opening just as Sam had done. A jean-and-
sweater-clad young man who appeared to be somewhere
in his twenties, cursed fluently as he burst through,
bits of hedge adding festive decorations to his clothing
and his full, somewhat tangled brown beard.

"Hey, thanks for grabbing the mutt," he panted as the
hedge finally released him. Then he did an obvious double take, merry blue eyes looking Lacy over with friendly
masculine appreciation. "Well, hello," he said, his greet-
ing drawled. "Are you a friend of Lynn's?"

Taking an immediate liking to the young man, Lacy
smiled back at him. "Not exactly." She reached out to
pluck a twig from his beard.

"Thanks," he said cheerfully, looking at the twig in vague surprise. Then he grinned at her. "Well, whoever you are, you're welcome to join the party. Actually, we're supposed to be studying; we'll get around to that, I suppose." His wayward gaze shifted to the Mercedes. "Hey, nice car! Yours?"

Lacy gestured over her shoulder with a thumb. "No. His."

The merry blue eyes peered at Randall's rather stony face. "Ah, there is a definite family resemblance; you must be one of Lynn's brothers. Scott?" he hazarded.

"No," Randall said briefly.

Sam's owner nodded genially. "Then you're the other one." He reached out to relieve Lacy of the dog. "I'll tell Lynn you're here." The hedge swallowed him up again.

Lacy stared at the quivering shrubbery, biting her lip. She sneaked a glance at Randall's face, and a giggle escaped in spite of all her efforts. "Um, he's obviously not a connoisseur of classical music," she ventured.

Randall winced as another clash of rock music emanated from the house. "Obviously."

Lacy knew very well that Randall had grasped her meaning. The young man had been clearly unimpressed by the family's famous musician, and that delighted Lacy.

Randall came around the car and took her hand. "Come on. We're going to find out what the hell's going on."

"I take it this party's a bit . . . unexpected?" she asked solemnly.

"A bit," he agreed dryly. "The place is supposed to be empty at this time of year."

They avoided Sam and his owner's shortcut, following the hedge as it turned toward the house and revealed a walkway. Also revealed as they made the corner were three cars parked at the garage. The sight didn't appear to afford Randall any enjoyment.

"Damn."

Concerned with the approach of what promised to be a nice little confrontation, Lacy only absently noticed that the house was every bit as sprawling as its roof had indicated. She saw weathered cedar siding and wide windows; the window to the left of the double door provided a clear view of several young people sprawled in various positions on furniture and floor and talking animatedly.

Randall reached for the door just as it swung open. The young woman standing inside stared up at Randall for a moment, then stepped back and yelled over her shoulder, "Close the den door, Kelly!"

There was a thud to the left of the hall, the decibel level immediately dropped, and Randall and Lacy entered the house. Lynn closed the door behind them, giving Lacy a moment to study her.

Like Sam's owner had, Lacy instantly saw the family resemblance. Lynn was tall and slender. Her shoulder-length hair was as black as her brother's, and she shared his golden eyes and classically perfect features. She was absolutely beautiful.

"What are you doing here, Randall?" she asked, a bit uneasily, Lacy thought.

Randall ignored the question. "Lynn, what's going on? Why aren't you in school?"

His sister lifted her chin defiantly. "We're going to be here until the middle of next week. Exams are coming up, and we have to cram."

"That's not exactly what it sounds like you're doing," he noted dryly. "Do Mom and Dad know what's going on here?"

"Of course they know! And what business is it of yours? I'm of age, Randall, and this happens to be my house as much as it is yours!"

Lacy stepped neatly into the breach. "Hi, I'm Lacy Hamilton," she told the younger woman cheerfully.

Lynn abandoned her confrontation with Randall, smiling at Lacy and displaying an innately sunny disposition. "Hi. Did you come with the bear here?"

"For my sins, yes," Lacy said gravely.

Randall made a choking sound and was ignored by both women.

"Well," Lynn said, "the house is certainly big enough to hold us all. And there's plenty of food; we stocked up yesterday."

"There are only five bedrooms," Randall inserted stonily. "How many friends do you have here?"

Lynn glanced at him. "There are six of us, counting me. But don't worry—we only need three bedrooms." After this somewhat defiant comment, she looked back at Lacy while Randall lapsed into a silence that quivered in the air. "You don't happen to speak French, do you, Lacy?"

"As a matter of fact, yes."

"Great! If I don't pass my French exam, Dad says I can't go to Europe this summer. Could you possibly—?"

Lacy laughed. "Happy to."

"Oh, thanks! Randall, your bedroom and Mom and Dad's are both empty; take your pick." She turned away from them. "I've got to tell the guys about our new French coach. Tomorrow, we can—"

Whatever they could do tomorrow was lost as the opening door brought the decibel level to shattering heights and drowned out Lynn's words. The noise became bearable again as she disappeared into what seemed to be the den and closed the door behind her.

Before Randall could say a word, Lacy headed back outside for their luggage. He followed.

"Dammit. If there were a hotel nearby—"

"Nonsense. There are two extra bedrooms, remember?" Lacy had privately decided that the presence of Lynn's friends was just what Randall needed. She only hoped there was no classical music buff among them.

"Did she mean what I think she meant about the bedrooms?" Randall demanded as he opened the trunk of the Mercedes.

"She's twenty-one, Randall."

"She's a baby!"

Lacy leaned against a fender and smiled slightly. "I was only a few years older than that," she reminded him softly.

He looked up from the luggage, an arrested expression in his eyes. Some of the stiffness drained away from him. "Touché." His smile was crooked. "And that was a low blow."

"Truth usually is," she conceded gently.

He straightened and slammed the trunk shut. "Okay, okay. But if she's sleeping with that hairy—"

Lacy burst out laughing. "Randall, will you listen to yourself? You've just put an entire generation between you and your sister!"

"It seems one exists," he growled, a flicker of wry amusement showing on his face. "I'm going to feel like the male equivalent of a den mother around this bunch."

At that moment, Sam's owner burst through the hedge again and grabbed two suitcases. "Welcome to the party!"

he said breezily, then promptly vanished back into the greenery.

Again Lacy stared at the quivering bushes for a moment, then looked toward Randall. He was also staring after the bearded young man, and his expression was impossible to fathom. After a long moment, he spoke in a considering tone. "On second thought, I won't feel like a den mother. Zookeeper is closer to the mark."

Lacy was still giggling as she followed him back into the house. They didn't take the shortcut.

Once inside, they discovered that the music had stopped—for the moment, at least—and introductions were performed. Lacy was amused to see that the other two young men were also bearded and that they showed an attitude of friendly insouciance toward the newcomers. Steve—no surnames were offered—was blond and athletic-looking, and Brian was the prototypical intellectual, complete with wire-rimmed glasses framing his mild brown eyes.

The young women were introduced as Lisa and Amy. Lisa was a tall redhead with green eyes and a good-humored smile; Amy was a petite blonde with freckles and an obvious habit of chewing gum.

Sam's owner, who reentered the hall after having apparently deposited the two suitcases somewhere, turned out to be Kelly. Judging by the way she held his hand as she introduced him to her brother and Lacy, Kelly was Lynn's man.

And Randall didn't look happy.

Lacy, always sensitive to undercurrents, watched Lynn closely as she introduced Kelly. She could see what Randall obviously had no awareness of: beneath the younger

woman's bland defiance was a need to win approval from
the big brother she had never really known.

Kelly, for his part, displayed a casual respect for Randall—whether because of his fame or because he was
Lynn's brother was impossible to say. Beneath his lighthearted manner, Lacy could sense easy self-confidence,
and she saw that his merry blue eyes were also sharp and
keenly intelligent.

Sam frisked about underfoot.

Lacy was immediately pelted with questions about her
mastery of French, and both Steve and Brian yelped with
relief when she admitted to knowing a bit of Latin as
well. A cheerful tussle ensued between the gals and guys
over who would benefit from Lacy's drilling first.

Randall plucked Lacy from the melee a few moments
later with a cool remark to his sister about the long drive
behind them. They were going to their rooms for a while,
he said, emphasizing the word *rooms*.

Glancing back as Randall led her toward the hall to
the right, Lacy saw that Lynn was staring after them and
biting her lip. Lacy smiled and winked at the younger
woman and was rewarded by a tentative smile from Lynn.

The house's five bedrooms were all in one wing, two
bedrooms on either side of the hall sharing a bathroom
between them. The master bedroom was at the end of
the hallway, and it was to that room that Randall led her.

The large room was decorated in shades of gold and
brown, with a thick pile carpet. The furniture was beautiful oak, a king-size bed occupying a central position.
Wide windows lent an airy spaciousness, and the wall
facing oceanward boasted glass doors opening onto a
wooden deck and commanding a spectacular view of the
sea.

Lacy looked at Randall. "Sure your parents won't mind?"

"Of course not." He glared toward the foot of the bed, where Kelly had placed their cases. "My room is the first to the left as you're leaving this one."

She followed his glare and hid a smile. "Kelly obviously thought we'd be sharing a room."

"Obviously," Randall grunted.

"Randall . . ." Lacy moved slowly to stand before him. "How long has it been since you've seen Lynn? Before today."

"Last summer."

"You didn't see her at Christmas?"

"No. I had a concert."

Frowning slightly, Lacy realized that there had been no show of affection between Randall and his sister. And they hadn't seen one another in nearly a year? Was Randall normally a demonstrative man? She didn't know. Lynn had struck her as being an affectionate woman, but there had been no hug or kiss—in fact, no touching at all.

A fourteen-year gap in age didn't explain that, Lacy thought. The distance between Randall and Lynn was made up of more than years.

"I'm sorry about this, Lacy," he was saying irritably. "Those kids had no right to rope you into drilling them. I'll have a talk with Lynn, and—"

"Randall." She smiled up at him. "I don't mind; I wouldn't have offered otherwise. It'll be fun."

He looked down at her, his eyes suddenly probing. "You're glad they're here, aren't you?" She simply continued to smile. "Why? Because their presence will . . . cramp my style?" he demanded.

Lacy heard the touch of bitterness in his deep voice, but she heard other things as well. She heard the shaken note of a man faced with the inescapable knowledge that his little sister was a grown woman—and a stranger to him. And she wondered if she heard the sound of weariness compounded of too many years of being a legend instead of a man.

She stepped even closer and slipped her arms around his waist. "First, I still think we need some time to get to know one another. And second..." She grinned up at him. "Their presence doesn't bother me a bit. Don't let it bother you."

Randall's hands tentatively kneaded her shoulders. His head bent toward hers, golden eyes darkening to honey, and she heard him catch his breath.

Then she heard a thump as the half-closed bedroom door was thrust open.

"Oops! 'Scuse me!" It was Kelly, jovially apologetic for his inopportune timing. "We're planning to barbecue ribs out back. You two hungry?"

Lacy hastily placed three fingers over Randall's lips to silence what promised to be a blistering response. "Starved," she answered cheerfully.

"Great!" Kelly vanished back down the hall.

She dropped her hand as Randall released her and stepped back. She watched as he stared after Kelly. And when he looked at her again, there was more than a hint of wrathful fire in his eyes.

"I bring you all the way out here so we can be alone together, and when we get here...It bothers me," he said flatly, obviously referring to the presence of Lynn and her friends. "It definitely bothers me."

"Why? You've always been in the public eye."

"Not with my clothes off!" he retorted, and, bending, he picked up his suitcase and stalked from the room.

CHAPTER
Six

LACY'S BELIEF THAT Lynn's friends were just what Randall needed wasn't noticeably borne out during the barbecue. It might have been the earlier interruption, or it might have simply been a culmination of a highly emotional and stress-ridden week. Whatever the reason, Randall's stiffness made absolutely no impact on the good-natured "kids."

Lowering skies and a damp breeze notwithstanding, they had a ball.

"Hey! Who's got the water bottle? The flames are climbing here!"

"Amy, where's the sauce?"

"Who's got the turner-thing?"

"That's 'spatula,' dummy."

"Is it? Well, who's got it?"

"Sam, I think. Sam? Sam!"

"What's Sam doing with it? He can't even reach the barbecue. No, don't hand it to me! Wash it first. I *know* Sam has fewer germs in his mouth than I have, but— Sam! Come back here with that rib, you mutt!"

"Let him have it. Can't you see the poor dog's starving?"

"He was born with begging eyes."

"So were you, and just see how far it's taken you."

"That's not funny, Lisa!"

"You have no sense of humor. Lacy, I want your recipe for this sauce."

"In English or French?"

"Whichever. Where's Lynn?"

"Here I am. We forgot the stuff for salad, guys."

"We have bread, don't we? I demand bread."

"Shut up, Kelly."

"Bread? Bread for a starving man?"

"Walk around with your hand out; maybe someone will take pity and give you a crust."

"Heartless wench."

"Hey! The ribs are being consumed by fire! Water bottle!"

"Stop howling; here it is."

"I've lost the turner—spatula again, dammit."

"Sam has it."

"Sam! Kelly, if you don't lock that mutt up—"

"It's bare bodkins at dawn, pal, if you criticize my dog."

"Bare what?"

"Don't mind him, Steve. He just likes to confuse you."

"My favorite pastime."

"Bare what?"

"Potato salad? Lacy, you're a doll!"

"Bare *what?*"

"Kelly, for God's sake, explain 'bodkins' to him!"

"Why? He never explains football to me."

"You *know* football."

"Details, details."

"This whole thing is *infra dignitatem*. Beneath my dignity to you morons. Lacy just taught me that."

"Amy, will you do something with Brian? He's muttering in Latin."

"I wasn't muttering."

"Water bottle!"

"Steve, stop howling! Here it is."

"Why am I cooking, anyway?"

"The apron fits you."

"Oh. Where's Sam?"

"Over there. Can't you see him? He's being a perfect gentleman."

"Well, where's the spatula?"

"I think he buried it."

"Oh, Lord!"

Lacy commandeered both the kitchen and Randall's help in making the potato salad. Although he still seemed stiff and uncommunicative with Lynn's friends, Lacy had seen his lips twitch more than once, and she felt hope. He'd never been granted their kind of irresponsible youth; Lacy didn't think he'd ever been allowed to be just a kid.

She wondered if Lynn knew that.

"Here, put these eggs on to boil."

"Yes, ma'am."

"And loosen your tie, Randall."

"I'm not wearing a tie."

"Really? I could have sworn something was choking you."

"Funny." Randall busied himself with starting the eggs, casting an occasional thoughtful glance her way. "You like these kids, don't you?"

"Sure do."

"Why?"

"Why not? They're nice, normal kids."

"They're nuts, every one of them."

"I like nuts."

Randall located a knife and began helping her peel potatoes. "I'm not a nut."

"No..."

"But?"

"But I also like messed-up piano players."

"Messed-up?"

"Are you fishing, Randall?"

"Desperately."

"Oh. Well, then—you've been working too hard all your life, Randall. You have to learn to play."

"Is that the answer to my question?"

"Definitely." She sent him a sidelong glance. "Forget music. Forget discipline. Relax. Unbend."

Randall sighed and went to dump the potato peelings into the trash can behind the door. Just as he turned back, the door burst open, nearly flattening him against the wall, and Kelly breezed in.

"Hi! Where's the bear?" he demanded cheerfully.

The door crashed shut behind him.

"Right behind you," Randall growled.

Kelly did an exaggerated double take and grabbed the

edge of the counter for support. "Oh, no! You let him off his leash!" he howled to Lacy. "Has he had all his shots?"

Lacy was laughing too hard to answer.

"Did you want something?" Randall asked pointedly.

"Take pity on a man having a heart attack here; I'll remember what I wanted in a minute," Kelly panted. "Lord! Didn't anyone ever teach you not to slam doors behind unsuspecting people?"

"Didn't anyone ever teach *you* to enter a room in a normal fashion?" Randall countered sardonically.

"My mother tried," Kelly replied seriously. "Needless to say, I went to bed many a night without my supper. Supper. Ah! Now I remember. We seem to have permanently misplaced the spatula. Lynn says there's a spare. You wouldn't happen to know..."

Randall went to one of the cabinets and rummaged for a moment, finally producing another long-handled barbecue spatula. He handed it to Kelly.

"Many thanks. I'd salaam, but I never mastered that, either."

"A loss to Oriental connoisseurs everywhere, I'm sure," Randall offered politely.

"He knows what a salaam is. Wonderful. An educated bear. I'll have to watch my step." Saluting them with the spatula, Kelly breezed back out.

Randall stared after him for a moment, and then his lips twitched. "Likeable kid," he murmured finally.

"Uh-huh." Lacy knew when *not* to go overboard with enthusiasm.

Wandering over to where Lacy was putting the potatoes on to boil, Randall appeared thoughtful. "Do you think it's serious between him and Lynn?"

Lacy checked the eggs. "I'd say so. But an outsider never really knows."

"True." He leaned back against the counter beside the stove, watching her. And he suddenly laughed. "This is not quite the image I had of our time together, Lacy."

"I'm sure!" She grinned at him.

He reached out to touch her cheek. "I counted on having you all to myself."

"Listen to the man—seduction on his mind."

"Objections?" he inquired lightly.

"If I said no, would that make me a scarlet woman?" she asked, a sudden unsteadiness in her voice.

His eyes darkened with riveting speed. "Dammit, Lacy," he murmured huskily. "Don't say that when—"

"Oh, horrors—I've done it again!" moaned a harried voice from the doorway. "Apologies, sincere apologies! I have rotten timing!"

Randall directed his gaze to where a woeful bearded face was peering around the half-open door. "You certainly have," he told Kelly affably. "And if you do it again, I shall strangle you with my bare hands—no pun intended."

Kelly blinked at him. "You would, too. I'll *bear* that in mind—no pun intended."

Lacy started laughing. "I'd like to make a pun just to keep my hand in!" she said wryly.

Randall bit back a laugh, then lifted a brow at the younger man. "Well? What now?"

"My, he's daunting, isn't he?" Kelly said seriously to Lacy. "What do you feed him? Gunpowder?"

"Only on weekends," she replied solemnly.

"Stop talking about me as if I weren't here!" Randall ordered, clearly harassed.

"Apologies again!" Kelly offered hastily.

"Well?"

Kelly blinked. "Well what?"

"What do you want?" Randall roared.

"No need to yell," Kelly murmured, wincing.

There was a faintly desperate gleam in Randall's eyes. He made an obvious effort. "Excuse me," he said carefully. "I get very cranky when I haven't had my nap."

Kelly nodded in an understanding manner while Lacy struggled with laughter. "I'm that way myself," he said sympathetically.

Randall held up a reproving finger. "You didn't let me finish."

"Sorry. You were saying?"

"I was just going to add a friendly warning. I'm cranky when I haven't had my nap. And I lean toward homicidal tendencies when interrupted by bearded students who burst through doors. Or even when they don't. I trust the warning is taken in the spirit in which it's given?"

Kelly tilted his head to one side. "What about professors?"

"What about them?"

"Does the warning apply to bearded professors who burst through doors?"

Randall stared at him for a long moment. "You don't mean—"

"'Fraid so. I'm a professor."

Randall's sigh held the sound of an overflowing cup. "Figures. Yes, the warning applies to professors."

"In that case, I'll be brief."

"I somehow doubt that," Randall murmured.

"Yes. Well. I was just wondering, Randall—You don't mind if I get familiar here, do you?"

"I don't mind if you get verbally familiar," Randall deadpanned.

Lacy choked, and there was a gleam of laughter in Kelly's eyes.

"Fine. Um, just for the record, I hadn't planned on any other kind of familiarity."

"That's good," Randall told him cordially.

"Uh-huh. Well, Randall, you wouldn't happen to know where we can find a shovel, would you?"

Randall blinked. "I seem to have lost the thread of this conversation."

"There never was one!" Lacy gasped.

Kelly grinned at them. "It's Sam. He seems to have gotten himself stuck in a hole. We have to dig him out."

"We?"

"Well, me. Unless you like digging dogs out of holes."

"I won't touch that remark."

"I didn't think you would. The shovel?"

Randall sighed. "In the tool shed by the garage."

"Thanks." Kelly ducked back outside.

Looking at Lacy with a gravity belied by the laughter in his eyes, Randall said, "I just lost all my faith in our educational system."

Mopping her streaming eyes with a dish towel, Lacy saw Randall heading for the door. "Where are you going?" she managed weakly.

"Are you kidding? This I have to see."

Laughing, Lacy turned back to her cooking as the door closed behind him. Randall was beginning to unbend, she decided happily. And by the time he helped dig that lovable mutt out—and she had every faith in Kelly's ability to talk him into doing just that—the last of his stiffness with Lynn's friends would be a thing of the past.

It was a first step. A giant one.

Sudden darkness and a chill rain caught the merry-makers by surprise a short while later, and the slightly damp meal was eaten inside in the casual dining room.

"These ribs are underdone, Steve."

"Well, don't blame me. I only cooked because the apron fit."

"He sounds aggrieved."

"He is aggrieved. And adroit. And astute. And—"

"No word games at the table, please."

"I was just going to add that Steve is also aloof. However, since we need all the loofs we can get—"

"Someone hit him with a roll. Not that one, dammit—it's mine!"

"Amy, give Kelly back his roll. He's been crowing about bread all day."

"Two hours do not a day make."

"Shut up, Kelly."

"Steve's still sulking. Why is Steve sulking?"

"Because Randall and I found three ribs in the hole with Sam."

"And Steve took it as a personal affront?"

"Apparently."

"I'm not sulking."

"Pouting, then."

"This ear of corn's raw!"

"We found that in the hole with Sam and the ribs, too."

"What!"

"I'm kidding, I'm kidding."

"You should have buried *him* in the hole, Randall."

"I told him that witty people died young."

"Anybody want a raw ear of corn?"

"Ex post facto."

"Brian's talking in Latin again. What did he say, Lacy?"

"After the deed."

"What's that got to do with anything?"

"Ask Brian."

"I'm afraid to hear his answer. Lacy, can you teach me some lovely gutter French?"

"If I say yes, you'll wonder where I learned it."

"From Randall, probably. Randall, can you speak French?"

"I can avoid ordering snails in a restaurant."

"Wonderful. That'll get you far."

"You'd be surprised."

"I doubt it."

"Are you sure you're a professor?"

"Do you play the piano?"

"I try."

"Well, I try to be a professor."

"You look like a kid."

"A thirty-year-old kid."

"You can't be thirty!"

"I swear. I'd show you my driver's license, except that Lynn confiscated it."

"Why?"

"She didn't want me driving up here."

"He's a lousy driver."

"Eat your raw corn, Lynn."

"I gave it to Amy."

"She likes raw corn?"

"So she says."

"Amy, do you like raw corn?"

"Shut up, Kelly."

The meal ended with a communal clean-up in the thankfully large kitchen, accompanied by the talkative chaos Lacy had come to expect from the cheerful bunch. She was delighted to see that Randall was no longer stiff—though obviously still a bit bemused. And although he appeared slightly uncomfortable with his sister, Randall seemed to be working toward an excellent understanding with the others—particularly Kelly.

"Hey, piano player!"

"Professor?"

"There's no dishwasher!"

"No kidding, Sherlock?"

"Well, why?"

"So you'll have to wash the dishes."

"That's not funny!"

"Am I laughing?"

"Somebody hit Randall for me."

"Wash the dishes, Kelly."

"Hey, wait! How did I get elected?"

"You're standing in front of the sink."

"Let the piano player do it; it's his house."

"I can't."

"Why not?"

"I'd ruin my hands."

"Now *that's* a convenient excuse!"

"Randall, you dry."

"Lacy!"

"Kelly can wash, and you dry."

"What're you going to do?"

"Supervise."

"She'll make somebody a nice shrew one day, won't she?"

"Shut up, professor."

"Everybody's always telling me to shut up."

"Take the hint."

"Steve? Where's Steve?"

"Hiding behind the door."

"Steve! Why aren't you helping?"

"Too many cooks spoil the broth."

"We're not cooking; we're cleaning! Help."

"Are the dishes insured?"

"Somebody give Steve something to do."

"Let him feed Sam."

"Oh, no! The last time I did that, I nearly lost a finger!"

"Flagrante delicto."

"Brian's talking Latin again. Lacy?"

"He said 'during the commission of the crime.'"

"Let's stuff a dish towel into his mouth."

"I'll hold your coat."

"I'll sit on him."

"Run for your life, Brian!"

"Amy!"

"Well, you're driving me crazy, too."

"No haven with the woman I love? What's the world coming to?"

"It went to hell in a bucket. Don't you read the newspapers?"

"Lisa, what're you doing?"

"Giving Steve something to do. Obviously."

"Stand with his arm around you? Gee, that's a big help."

"Take that silly grin off your face, Steve."

"This isn't a grin."

"Smirk, then."

"Wrong again."

"Well, whatever it is, get rid of it!"

"Let Steve take out the garbage."

"I can't leave Lisa all alone!"

"We'll comfort her while you're gone."

"Bare bodkins at dawn, Kelly, if you touch my lady."

"Bare bodkins! That's obscene!"

"He's trying to confuse you again, Steve."

"Dammit, Kelly!"

"Somebody call the police! This bearded creature has just threatened me with an obscenity!"

"Shut up, Kelly."

"The piano player will defend me from all this abuse. Won't you, piano player?"

"Of course I will."

"That grin was more teeth than humor. I don't trust you, piano player. You'd sit on me and let them beat me up, wouldn't you?"

"I have to protect my hands, you see."

"Ahhh! Piano player! I'd thought better of you!"

"That'll teach you to think, professor."

"Will someone tell me what a bodkin is?"

"Lacy, why are you sitting on the counter?"

"The traffic was getting dangerous."

"Well, while you're sitting there, put these plates away."

"Yes, sir."

"He'll make somebody a nice shrew one day, too, won't he?"

"Shut up, professor."

"Bodkin?"

"Hey, you missed a spot."

"Don't criticize, piano player, unless you're prepared to do the thing yourself."

"Wash it again."

"I will not."

"Then *you'll* eat off of it tomorrow."

"Why didn't you say so in the first place? I'll wash it again."

"Bodkin?!"

"Dagger, Steve."

"What?"

"A bodkin is a dagger. Remember Shakespeare?"

"He never met him."

"Shut up, Kelly."

"A dagger?"

"A dagger."

"Thanks, Lacy."

"Don't mention it."

"Ouch! Who hit me?"

"Just pick anybody, Kelly."

"It was Steve! Is that the hem of your guilt showing, Steve?"

"Shut up, Kelly. You deserve it."

"Lynn!"

"What?"

"You're supposed to defend me!"

"If Steve wants to beat you up, I'll hold his coat."

"Piano player?"

"I'll hold his watch. Wouldn't want the crystal to get shattered."

"Lacy?"

"I always did love a good fight."

"I didn't come all this way to be abused, guys. I could have stayed at home and gotten that."

"Lacy, where's the bucket of tar?"

"It's in the cabinet here, all ready."

"Who's got the feathers?"

"Hey!"

"Randall put them behind the door. Let's see . . ."

"Hey!!"

Somebody suggested popcorn after the clean-up, and eight healthy appetites thought that was a good idea. Randall unearthed several old-fashioned corn poppers and built a fire in the den fireplace, assisted by a critical Kelly.

Lacy had only vaguely noticed the den before, but she saw now that it contained a baby-grand piano. The piano was in a corner flanked by two wide windows providing what would be a lovely view in daylight. Two couches, a loveseat, and two chairs were grouped about the rustic stone fireplace. In the corner between the windows and behind the piano, she saw a huge trophy case containing an impressive collection of medals and trophies—Randall's, she knew.

He never even glanced toward that corner.

Lacy sat down in one corner of the loveseat and watched the amiable argument going on over who would hold the corn poppers. When Randall came to sit down beside her, it felt entirely natural for him to put an arm around her and draw her close to his side.

Relaxed and pleasantly weary herself, Lacy noted with gratitude the amusement on Randall's face as he listened to the kids. To see that look on his face, she would have been willing to drill an entire college in French and Latin.

The argument was finally settled, leaving Kelly, Steve, and Lynn holding the poppers over the fire. Amy and Brian shared one of the couches, and Lisa joined Steve. Sam curled up contentedly in a chair. A companionable silence filled the room, and it apparently became too much for the irrepressible Kelly.

"Let's play charades!"

Leaning back against him, Lynn groaned. "Let's sit in blissful silence; it'll be a nice change."

"Twenty questions?"

"Somebody gag that man."

Kelly sighed. "Spoilsports."

"You're hyper, professor."

"I am that, piano player."

"What're you professor *of,* by the way?"

"Psychology. So hold on to your id."

"I thought Freud was passé," Randall murmured.

"He'll rise up from his grave and get you for that."

"He'll probably get *you.*"

"I'm going to hate myself for this, but I'll bite, piano player. Why will Freud get me?"

"Because you're a blot on his cherished profession."

"I knew I'd hate myself."

"Kelly, you're spilling your corn!"

"Hey, mine's done," Steve said suddenly. "Bowls! We need bowls. And butter and salt—"

"Stop howling, Steve!"

There was a general rush to acquire bowls, salt, and

butter, and the popcorn was duly seasoned and doled out.
Kelly and Lynn remained seated by the hearth, while
Steve and Amy appropriated the unoccupied couch. Conversation went by the board for a while, and the crackle
of the fire and the crunch of popcorn being consumed
were the only sounds.

Lynn finally stirred slightly. "Why don't you play for
us, Randall?"

Stealing a quick glance at Randall's face, Lacy saw
it tighten slightly, and she wished suddenly than anyone
but Lynn had made the suggestion. She was bound to be
hurt when—

"Not tonight," Randall said easily, staring past his
sister and into the orange flames.

Lacy saw Lynn bite her lip and wished she could say
something to make the younger woman feel better. But
she couldn't. Her gaze shifted to Kelly, and she saw that
he was looking from Randall's face to her own, his eyes
keen and thoughtful.

And it was Kelly who stepped into the breach and
prevented any of the others from asking Randall to play.

"I'll tell you all a story."

"If it's one of your dirty limericks," Brian said, "we
don't want to hear it."

"Speak for yourself," Steve advised.

"Steve likes locker-room humor," Brian muttered.

"Come on, guys—listen up."

"We're a captive audience, professor," Randall said
in amusement.

"I'll say," Lisa bemoaned. "In this weather, who can
leave?"

"Once upon a time—" Kelly began firmly.

"Is this a fairy tale?" Steve demanded.

"Shut up. Once upon a time, there was a castle. And in this castle lived a king..."

The story went on. It was filled with knights and dragons and maidens in distress and lots of delightful nonsense. Kelly's voice was soft and oddly lyrical, weaving a spell in the firelit room. A curiously romantic spell.

And Kelly didn't seem to mind that half his audience had quietly left the room before the end of the story, leaving only him and Lynn and Randall and Lacy. When he finished with "and they lived happily ever after," he rose to his feet and pulled Lynn gently to hers.

"Good night, you two."

"Good night," Randall and Lacy both murmured. They watched as the younger couple and Sam left the room.

CHAPTER
Seven

"I STILL LOVE YOU, you know."

The quiet words came out of the firelit silence of the room, and Lacy felt her heart begin to pound almost painfully. Her soft laugh was more than a little shaky. "Kelly's story got to you."

"No." Randall slid his free arm beneath her knees, lifting her easily until she was lying across his lap. He gazed at her with honey eyes. "No."

The ache inside Lacy grew until it hurt even to breathe. She watched her arms slide up around his neck, hearing a dim voice in her head warning her of prices to be paid. She didn't listen. She didn't want to listen.

"Randall . . ."

"Shhh." His lips feathered lightly along her jawline in a touch no heavier than dew. One hand slipped beneath

115

her bulky sweater to lie warmly against her narrow waist. "I know you want time. But don't hate me for needing to touch you," he whispered.

She locked her fingers in his silky black hair as his lips hovered over hers, and it was Lacy who made the final movement, closing the distance between them in sudden heedless need.

Randall pulled her fiercely against him, one hand tangled in her fine hair and the other sliding around to move probingly up and down her spine. He kissed her as though some inner urgency commanded it, as though the taste of her fed some desperate hunger.

And Lacy couldn't help but respond. Her senses whirled and tumbled in a mindless vacuum; her upper body molded itself to his in an effort to be closer to him, a part of him. The faint voice of reason moaned a last plea for sanity and was ruthlessly banished.

His lips left hers finally, reluctantly, and she kept her eyes closed as he rained fiery kisses on her upturned face. Her fingers probed the tension-knotted muscles at the nape of his neck, digging in suddenly when his hand slid up beneath her sweater to warmly cup her breast.

Lacy gasped, feeling her nipple swell and harden, feeling a spreading empty ache in her middle.

"Lacy," he whispered hoarsely, his fingers shaping willing flesh. "My Lacy."

She lifted heavy eyelids to look at him, seeing his own eyes honey-dark and compelling. The siren song was in those eyes again, calling to her in the sweetest voice this side of heaven. And she was willing to dash herself against the rocks to obey that voice.

Her fingers tangled once again in his hair as she sought his mouth with her own, arching her body against his with the instincts of ages. Tongues met, battled furiously. She trembled, feeling the responding shudder in his lean frame, and the desire inside her spiraled crazily.

"Lacy!" Her name was a rasping sound, seemingly torn from his throat when he wrenched his mouth from hers, and she could feel his heart thundering against her. "Are you sure?" he demanded thickly.

Mindlessly, she allowed her lips to feather along his jawline, wondering why he was talking. "It doesn't matter," she whispered feverishly, needing him to take her to bed and make love to her until it really didn't matter. She wanted tonight... even if that was all she would have in the end.

But the hand still tangled in her hair gently forced her face into the curve of his shoulder, and his arms held her tightly against him, preventing her instinctive explorations. "It matters," he grated softly, his breathing still harsh and empty. "Oh, how it matters. I can't lose you again, honey. And if you aren't sure... I'll lose you."

Lacy breathed in his clean masculine scent, feeling the pulse pounding in his neck. Her desire slowly, painfully abated. She was aware of his hand stroking up and down her spine beneath the sweater, comforting, undemanding, and emptiness ached in her. "Randall..." she murmured, hearing in her own voice the note of a lost little girl.

"They say self-denial builds character," he said with an unsteady laugh.

Regaining her composure with an effort, Lacy straightened in his lap and met his still-darkened eyes hesitantly. She loved him more in that moment than she ever had, and it took all her strength to keep it out of her eyes. Reaching desperately for a light note, she managed a reproving tone. "You're being awfully noble."

Randall clearly approved of the lighter atmosphere. "Just trying to build my character, love."

"Is that what you're doing?"

"Obviously."

"Oh. Just how tall are you going to build it? Empire State Building size?" she suggested with real amusement.

He winced. "I don't think I'll be able to rise to the heights demanded of me."

Lacy started laughing. "That's a terrible pun!"

"Have a little sympathy," he requested wryly. "It's a miracle I can make even a bad pun in my condition."

There was a sudden soft pop as what was left of the fire fell in on itself, catching their attention. "The fire's going out," Lacy observed, needing to say something.

"I'll bank it for the night." He rose, still holding her, and then set her gently on her feet. "You go on to bed; it's been a long day."

Lacy nodded and turned away from him, heading toward the doorway. Once there, she halted and half turned back. Randall was standing by the fireplace, watching her.

"Randall?"

"Hmmm?"

"You're not very comfortable with Lynn, are you?"

He lifted a brow at her. "When you change the subject, you really do it, don't you?"

"Are you?" she repeated steadily.

"No." He shook his head slightly. "No, I'm not."

"She's your sister."

"She's a stranger, Lacy. I don't know her."

"Kelly was more of a stranger, but you're comfortable with him."

Randall shrugged. "I can't explain it."

"I can." Lacy's smile was wry. "Kelly didn't grow up with a legend for an older brother."

There was an arrested expression in Randall's eyes. "And Lynn did."

"Lynn did." Lacy hesitated for a moment. "Randall, you grew up inside the spotlight; Lynn grew up just outside it. And that couldn't have been easy for her."

"No." Randall was staring into the dim red glow of the fire.

Lacy studied him for a moment and then, satisfied, nodded slightly. "Good night, Randall."

"Good night, love."

She went from the den and through the entrance hall to the bedroom wing of the house. The hall was dimly lit, and she had no trouble locating her bedroom. She went in and switched on the light, closing the door softly behind her. She spent a few minutes unpacking—something she'd had little time for until now—and then took a shower in the lovely green and yellow bathroom.

Lying on the wide bed a while later, Lacy stared into the darkness and tried to think about the day. But her thoughts kept taking abrupt turns and made little sense. Each path wound inexporably back to the interlude on the couch—and Randall's determination for her to be sure of what she was doing. This time.

But what Randall didn't know—what she couldn't tell him—was that her love for him made her even more vulnerable this time around. Because she knew now what she stood to lose by loving him.

She couldn't share a legend with the world. She just couldn't.

* * *

Lacy was faintly surprised when she woke up early
the next morning, since she hadn't left a mental reminder
to herself to do so. Her travel clock showed the time to
be just after seven, and the light coming through the
windows advertised an overcast day.

And somebody began playing the piano.

Lacy stiffened for a moment in the bed, listening
intently. Then she relaxed. It wasn't Randall. She knew
his gifted touch, and this musician, although more than
adequate, didn't begin to compare.

She slid from the bed and made it neatly, then dressed
in jeans and a bright green cowl-neck sweater. Except
for a touch of lipstick, she didn't bother with makeup.
With only a little coaxing, her black hair fell neatly into
its usual casual style.

Leaving her bedroom, she noted that all the other
doors were open, the beds made, and the rooms neat and
empty. And, other than the distant strains of a Mozart
piano sonata, the house was silent.

Lacy stole quietly through the entrance hall and into
the den, stopping just inside the doorway.

Lynn was alone in the room, playing the piano with
an absentminded air as she gazed out through one of the
windows. She was dressed casually in an unbuttoned
flannel shirt worn over a knit top and jeans. She seemed
unaware of Lacy's presence for a few moments, then
broke off abruptly and turned on the bench to stare toward
the doorway.

Moving toward her, Lacy said, "I'm sorry. I didn't
mean to startle you."

"You didn't." Lynn shrugged. "Hope I didn't wake
you up; Randall would have a fit."

Lacy stopped beside the piano. "I was awake before

you started playing. Where are the others?"

"Out hunting shells, if you can believe that at seven-thirty. They haven't even had breakfast."

"Randall, too?" Lacy was surprised.

Lynn smiled. "Kelly challenged him. You know—who could find the best shell? Randall fell for it."

With a laugh, Lacy said, "Good for Kelly! He's a nice guy, Lynn."

"He's not my professor," Lynn said suddenly, a trace of defiance in her voice. "I mean, I don't take any of his classes. I wouldn't get involved with one of my own professors."

Lacy looked at her for a moment, and then sat down on the bench as Lynn moved over to make room for her. "I'd say that was a wise decision," she told the younger woman mildly.

Lynn nodded jerkily. "Does—does Randall know?"

"Even if he doesn't," Lacy said slowly, "he wouldn't judge you."

"Wouldn't he just!" Lynn's laugh was hollow and older than her years. She brought her hand down suddenly on the keys in a crash of discordant sound. "I never could measure up. Never! I could never be more than average."

"You mean musically?"

"Musically . . . and everything else."

Seeking to comfort, Lacy told her. "You're certainly not average in looks; you're a beautiful woman."

Lynn sent her a wry glance. "I don't mean to sound conceited, but looks run in my family. I'm average in that, too. I don't stand out."

"You want to stand out?"

"In something." Absently, Lynn picked out a simple

tune with one finger. "When I was small, I wanted to
be just like Randall. I wanted to play music and hear
applause. But I wasn't good enough."

Lacy thought of Randall's remark that neither his
brother nor sister had ever competed "or wanted to." She
sighed. "We can't all be that gifted," she said gently.

Lynn shrugged and fell silent for a moment, then she
blurted out, "Randall was special! All my life he was
special. He was usually on tour or competing somewhere,
and when he was home Scott and I weren't allowed to
disturb him. Scott was my brother, but Randall...
Randall was someone else. Someone I couldn't touch.
And I was jealous of the whole world—because they
had him and I didn't!"

Lacy understood. Oh, how she understood! A sister
and a lover, she thought, both trying desperately to love
a legend. But recently, the lover had learned a little and
Lacy had to share that awareness with the sister who was
still searching blindly.

"Randall was cheated out of a lot," she said quietly.

"But he's famous!" Lynn protested.

"Yes, he is. He earned that fame. And he had to pay
for it, Lynn."

The younger woman looked at her, puzzled. "But... the
rewards..."

"What rewards? Applause? That never mattered to
Randall. Being the best? He never thought he was the
best. What rewards did he have, Lynn?"

Lynn remained silent.

Lacy went on quietly. "He didn't have a childhood.
From the age of five, he worked. Sure, he worked at
something he loved. And that's a reward of sorts, I suppose. He learned discipline and concentration, and he
heard applause." She gestured toward the trophy case

behind them. "He won trophies and medals. He saw concert halls in every major city in the world. But he never had the time to see the cities themselves. And he never enjoyed the applause because while it was ringing in his ears, he was mentally going over his performance and silently damning himself for the tiny mistake only he heard."

Lynn said nothing, though her quizzical look spoke volumes to Lacy.

Lacy continued. "You said it yourself, Lynn. Randall was 'special.' And for 'special,' read 'different'— 'apart'—'alone.' He became a legend, and the world embraced him . . . from a distance. People tend to want their legends on a pedestal, well out of reach. They want surface glitter, and they demand perfection. They're so blinded by the star that they never see the man behind it." Her voice deepened in pain, the last sentence an accusation aimed at herself.

Lynn rubbed the back of one hand across her eyes in a childlike gesture, wiping away tears. "No wonder he was never a brother," she whispered.

"He never learned how to be, Lynn. And he never had the time—then—to regret it. But he regrets it now."

"He—he looked shocked when he realized I was sleeping with Kelly."

"Of course he did. And it had nothing to do with morals. Randall was hit in the face with the knowledge that his little sister was a grown woman. He missed *your* childhood years as well as his own."

"You seem to understand him well." Lynn stared down at the keys.

"It took a while," Lacy said. "I was blinded by the glitter, too."

"How long have you known him?"

"We met about a year ago. I was his translator on that last European tour."

"Kick me if I'm being nosy"—Lynn smiled—"but were you and Randall . . . involved? Then, I mean?"

Lacy knew what she was asking. "For a while. A few months."

"What happened?"

"I was stupid, and I ran away." Months of inner misery, Lacy thought tiredly, neatly packaged into one small sentence.

"But you're trying again?"

"We're trying."

Lynn gazed at her steadily, obviously wanting to know but afraid to ask.

Hardly aware she was doing it, Lacy picked out a soft, sad tune with one hand. "I'm jealous of the whole world, too," she said softly. "And I don't know if I can cope with that."

"It's hell loving a celebrity, isn't it?" Lynn laughed a little shakily.

"It is indeed." Lacy gave the younger woman a sudden impulsive hug and was pleased when it was returned. "Now, what do you say we go start breakfast for the menagerie? Shell hunting is bound to give them all a whale of an appetite."

Lynn sighed ruefully. *"Everything* gives Kelly an appetite!"

When Kelly burst through the back door nearly an hour later, he was panting breathlessly and wearing a silly triumphant grin.

The appetizing scent of bacon filled the kitchen; Lacy and Lynn had worked together efficiently. Both looked up as the door nearly parted company with its hinges,

Lacy neatly flipping a pancake from the griddle onto a plate, and Lynn pouring juice into glasses.

"Kelly!" Lynn glared at him. "Can't you come into a room like any decent person?"

"I won!" he crowed happily.

"Won what?" she asked him with a long-suffering sigh.

"The race, my love. I challenged Randy."

Lacy's eyebrows rose, and she thought with amusement that anyone who had the nerve to shorten Randall's name was indeed a force to be reckoned with. "You're five years younger than he is," she pointed out mildly.

"Well, snatch the pleasure of my victory, why don't you?" Kelly gave her a look of mock annoyance.

"Sorry," she murmured.

"I *gave* him a five-yard start," Kelly told them virtuously.

"Liar," accused a deep, somewhat breathless voice from the doorway.

Unabashed, Kelly turned to grin at his competition. "Where've you been, piano player? I was about to go find a cardiac-care unit and look for your fallen body."

Randall was leaning against the doorjamb, dressed like Kelly in faded jeans and a sweatshirt. He raked a hand through his windblown hair, and then shook a fist under Kelly's nose. "You took a shortcut, you snake!"

"You did, too, or else you wouldn't have known that I did." Kelly snatched a strip of bacon from the plate on the counter and bit into it with relish, eyeing Randall with a complacent smile. "Footprints in the sand, piano player? It rained last night, you know."

"Speaking of rain," Lynn said wryly, "where's the rest of the storm?"

"They're coming," Randall answered, pushing himself away from the doorway and crossing the room to Lacy. To her astonishment, he kissed her lightly. "Hello."

"Hello," she murmured, hastily turning another pancake and wondering if she looked as startled as she felt. "Um, what happened to the shells you guys went after?"

Kelly offered an answer. "Randy jogged my elbow, and I dropped the two best specimens into a tidal pool," he said indignantly.

"I told you not to call me that," Randall countered mildly. "And I didn't jog your elbow; you tripped over your own feet."

"You're just sore because you lost the race."

"Want to make it best two out of three, professor—with no shortcuts?"

"After breakfast."

Lynn looked at Lacy with a smile of purely feminine amusement. "Do you get the feeling that these two are playing macho games?"

"It occurred to me." And Lacy was delighted by it; a little healthy male competition, she thought, wouldn't hurt Randall a bit.

"The contest is unequal to begin with," Kelly announced, filching another strip of bacon. "Randy doesn't have a beard."

"So?" Randall stared at him with one eyebrow on the rise.

"It's macho to have a beard." Kelly stroked his complacently with one hand. "Puts me ahead at least ten points in the game."

"Want us to leave the room while you boys thrash it out?" Lynn asked wryly.

"Do," Randall invited cordially, smiling gently at Kelly.

Kelly returned the stare for a moment, then caught Lynn's hand firmly. "Don't you dare. The piano player has an ace up his sleeve. I don't know what it is, but it's definitely there."

Randall looked piously innocent.

"What is it, piano player? Out with it!"

"Nothing much."

"Just?"

"Just a little karate. I started taking classes a few years ago."

"You'd hurt your hands," Kelly pointed out anxiously.

"I don't have to use my hands. My feet are lethal."

Lynn sent a glance of amusement at Kelly's stricken face. "With your shield or on it," she murmured.

"I'd rather not try it either way," Kelly told her hastily. "And stop putting ideas into your brother's head." He snatched a dish towel and waved it energetically. "I surrender, piano player. The battle's yours."

"What about the war?" Randall asked smoothly.

"You don't like half-measures, do you?"

"Let's just say I like clear victories."

Kelly sighed. "My white flag just waved again."

"Glad to hear it. Your penalty—"

"My *what?*" Kelly yelped.

"Penalty. You lost the war: you pay a penalty."

"Wonderful."

"Your penalty is that you have to wash the breakfast dishes."

"That's cruel and unusual punishment."

"Not at all. Besides, the sight of you up to your elbows in dishwater will afford me immense satisfaction."

"Sadist."

"My middle name."

Kelly appealed to Lynn with a hangdog look. "Sweetie, wouldn't you—"

"No. I helped cook."

"Heartless wench."

"I'll remember you said that."

"I can't win for losing!"

"'Fraid you're stuck, professor."

"Damn. Maybe one of the other—"

"I doubt it."

Kelly sighed. "Well, hell."

"Eureka!" howled a voice suddenly, and Steve came through the still-open door as though he'd been shot from a cannon. He halted his mad rush in the middle of the kitchen floor and looked rather hesitantly around at four determinedly stony faces.

"Hi," he offered, chagrin heavy in his voice. "I, um, I thought I'd try one of Kelly's entrances."

"It lost something in the translation," Kelly told him politely.

"Dammit, Kelly!"

Everyone but Steve was still laughing when the others trooped through the door. The source of their amusement was explained, and there was some good-natured teasing directed at Steve, who took it all with a sheepish smile.

Lacy, who had already realized that Steve deliberately played an excellent foil for Kelly's straight man, admired his composure. Not many men, she thought wryly, were secure enough in themselves to play the clown. She liked him. In fact, she liked them all. Their exuberant good humor was infectious.

"Hey, pancakes!"

"Do we have jelly? I love them with jelly."

"I don't know, but I'm carrying them to the table. If I don't, Kelly'll gobble 'em all up."

"That's slander!"

"Shut up, Kelly."

"I'll carry the bacon."

"No, you won't! You've already had two strips."

"Lacy, you cut me to the quick! I—"

"Never mind. Go and sit down at the table; you have to recruit your strength for the dishwashing, remember?"

"Kelly has to wash the dishes? How did that come about?"

"Never mind."

"Out with it, Kelly!"

"I said never mind!"

"He lost to Randall in the war."

"You're a traitor, Lynn!"

"War? What war?"

"It was in all the papers, dummy."

"Shut up, Kelly. What war, Lynn?"

"The macho war."

"And Kelly lost? Dear me."

"Wipe that grin off your face, Steve!"

"This isn't a grin."

"That's a Cheshire Cat grin if I've ever seen one!"

"Have you ever?"

"Ever what?"

"Seen one?"

"Ahhh!"

"Would someone please remove Kelly's fingers from my throat? I think he's hurting himself. Ah. Thank you, Randall."

"Don't mention it."

"Let go of me, piano player."

"Lethal feet, professor."

"Excuse me. *Please* let go of me."

"Better, but no cigar."

"At least you let go of me."

"For now."

"I hate veiled threats."

"Was that veiled?"

"You don't have to pull out my chair, piano player."

"I'm not being gallant, professor. I intend to see that you sit down and be quiet."

"He's being daunting again, Lacy!"

"You're on your own, Kelly."

"I have a host of friends."

"You'll have a host of mourners if you don't shut up."

"I'm constitutionally unable to shut up. Throw me a big wake, will you? Everybody get drunk and dance."

"Can I dance with Lynn?"

"If Lisa doesn't hit you for that, I will."

"I don't mind if he dances with Lynn. Once."

"That's my love."

"Eat your bacon, Steve."

"Yes, ma'am."

"I think her foot's planted firmly on your neck there, Steve!"

"Stuff a pancake in his mouth somebody."

"Don't you dare, piano player!"

"What was that, professor?"

"Okay, okay. I'm properly cowed. Now stop picking on me!"

"Did anyone see me picking on the professor?"

"Nope."

"Of course not."

"No way."

"Absolutely not."

"I didn't see a thing."

"What professor?"

"You were saying, professor?"

"A host of friends. I have a veritable host of friends . . ."

"E pluribus unum."

"Thank you, Brian."

"What did he say?"

"Steve, I'll grant that you could possibly be unfamiliar with Shakespeare, but don't try to tell me that you don't recognize your very own national motto!"

"Is that what he said?"

"Yes."

"In Latin?"

"Yes!"

"Well, no wonder I didn't recognize it!"

"Give me strength . . ."

"Who? I wouldn't give you the time of day."

"Is it my imagination, or are the puns getting worse?"

"And worse, and worse."

"Pass the toast, please."

"Coming your way."

"Who told Kelly that each piece of toast was a small Frisbee?"

"Want some bacon? I'm better with bacon. I can twist the strips, see, and make a little plane—"

"Stop throwing your food, children."

"Yes, Papa."

"I'd kill myself. Lacy, why're you laughing?"

"Your face! Sheer, unadulterated horror!"

"The piano player doesn't want to be my daddy? I'm hurt. I'm desperately, grievously hurt!"

In the confusion of the breakfast clean-up, Lacy found herself being pulled furtively from the kitchen and into the hall. Before she could do more than look at Randall in bemusement, he guided her into a closet and firmly pulled the door shut.

Lacy managed to hold on to her composure until he flipped the light switch on, but one look at Randall's satisfied expression toppled it.

"What in the world?" she gasped, laughing.

"Alone at last!" Randall pulled her even closer in the cramped closet, one eyebrow lifting in a creditable leer. "I refuse to share you all the time with that bunch of nuts!"

She slipped her arms around his waist and smiled up at him, delighted to see that even after the morning's exertions, much of the weariness she had come to dread had dissipated from his face. She was also delighted with his playfulness in pulling her into a closet, of all places!

"Well, now that you have me alone," she murmured seductively, "what are you going to do with me?"

"That's a loaded question," he warned huskily, his head bending toward hers.

The closet door was pulled abruptly open.

"Excuse me," Kelly told them politely. "I was looking for my coat." He peered around them, totally deadpan. "Hmmm. It must be in one of the other closets. Pardon me, I'm sure." Carefully, he turned off the light and gently shut the closet door.

Into the darkness, Lacy said shakily, "He... um... certainly has a way with doors."

Randall's voice was considering. "And interruptions. This is getting to be a habit."

"Now you know how I felt," she said, her voice still unsteady with laughter.

"You've made your point." Randall sighed. "And now I'm being punished."

"Punished?" She choked off a last giggle.

"Definitely. I'd hesitate to class that bearded nut as belonging in the real world, but it occurs to me that the interruptions are coming from your world now, honey— not mine."

"Yes, I've noticed. Ironic, isn't it?"

"Irritating."

"Uh-huh. Um, Randall?"

"Hmmm?"

"Are we going to stand here in the dark all day?"

"Well, something else just occurred to me."

"Really? What's that?"

"There's no graceful way to leave a closet."

Lacy broke apart. "Chin up!" she gasped.

"It's my tattered dignity I'm worried about."

"You shouldn't have pulled me in here."

"It seemed like a good idea at the time."

"But not now?"

"I've had better."

"Shall we leave?"

"I suppose we should. That bearded fruitcake certainly broke the mood."

"You first."

"I'll never live this down..."

CHAPTER
Eight

NO ONE OBSERVED their exit from the closet, although Lacy had a feeling Kelly would dearly love to have been there. They found the kids in the kitchen, having just finished with the cleaning chores. A coin was flipped solemnly, and Lacy retired to the den with Lynn, Lisa, and Amy for drilling in French. The men and Sam disappeared outside.

Over the next couple of days Lacy discovered that Lynn and her friends were in deadly earnest over their studies. Jokes were held to a minimum—even when it was Steve and Brian's turn for Latin—and close attention was paid to Lacy. As for herself, Lacy was at ease with the task. French was her strongest language, and since her father had possessed a lifelong interest in Latin, she was comfortable with it as well.

She also discovered—or rather, suspected—that Kelly, at least, had launched a determined campaign to keep her and Randall apart. Although she believed they needed to go slowly, Lacy had counted on spending *some* time alone with Randall. But she didn't try to stop Kelly's ceaseless interruptions, because he was making her point far better than she'd been able to do.

Randall was beginning to realize just how wearing interruptions could be on one's patience.

"I'm reduced to sneaking around—at my age!" Randall grumbled irritably just before lunch one day, after having finally managed to get Lacy alone in the den.

She looked at him innocently. "Oh, is that what you're doing? From that furtive look on your face, I thought you were planning to steal the silver. Ridiculous, really, since it belongs to you."

"Funny."

"Soup's on!" Kelly announced cheerfully from the doorway. And before Randall could wreak vengeance on him, he was gone again.

"He's worse than a cuckoo clock!" Randall said in a harassed voice.

Lacy was laughing. "Cuckoo clocks belong in the real world," she pointed out finally. "It looks like you and I can't live in either of our worlds!"

"I'm beginning to think so," Randall sighed, taking her hand and leading her toward the doorway. "Let's go eat. If we don't, he'll just find us again."

Ultimately Lacy was grateful for the breathing room Kelly's interruptions provided. It gave her time to do everything in her power to bring Randall and his sister closer together. And in that she was aided by the entire crowd, who seemed to sense, with young people's sometimes startling insight, that a gap needed bridging.

During breaks from cramming, games were begun on the beach or shell hunts launched or some other ultimately ridiculous amusement suggested. With surprising tact, the kids helped Lacy get Randall and his sister talking, and the absurdity of various games and contests made laughter a matter of course.

And Lacy was delighted by the results. Randall was clearly making an effort—first tentative, then gradually casual and brotherly—to get to know his sister. And Lynn's eagerness to spend time with the brother she'd never really known had paved the way.

The days slipped into a pattern. Mornings and afternoons were spent alternately with French and Latin, and whatever group was free always found something to do outside, usually on the beach. They played a spirited game of volleyball or threw Frisbees or just went exploring.

Lacy was reprieved from her duties periodically and drafted into a game of volleyball or touch football. Which led to some interesting encounters with Randall.

"We've got to stop meeting like this," she said with breathless solemnity after one gentle tackle.

"I know," he said, stealing a quick kiss, "but it seems to be the only time I can get you alone."

The rest of the group rushed toward them happily just then, and Randall saved Lacy from being crushed under a weight of enthusiasm only by quick thinking and even quicker reflexes. He threw the ball to Kelly. And the group tackled *him*.

* * *

The household duties of cooking and cleaning were always shared fairly equally and taken care of with undiminished good humor. And the group always finished the day with popcorn around the den fireplace, and usually a round of tall tales.

As for herself and Randall, Lacy found that she was torn by new insights into his character. He was relaxed and humorous now, his weariness completely gone. And he was making the effort to get to know his sister—and doing very well. Twenty-one years of brotherly neglect couldn't be made up for in a few short days, of course, but the turning point in their relationship was obvious. Randall was cheerful and casual with everyone—including Lacy.

She discovered, with some surprise, that he was indeed an openly demonstrative man. He held her hand and hugged her or kissed her with no apparent concern over who might be—and usually was—watching.

He'd probably decided, she thought wryly, to make the best of things.

At least that's what she thought until Randall pulled her aside during one of the communal clean-ups and whispered, "It's no good! You'll just have to creep into my room one night and seduce me!"

"I'll keep that in mind," she whispered back conspiratorially.

Lighthearted though Randall had seemed over the matter, Lacy was seriously beginning to consider seduction. A large part of her was still painfully worried about loving a star, but she had long ago passed the point of no return where he was concerned. Like the Little Mermaid who had shed her tail for feet, Lacy was willing to face tomorrow's pain tomorrow—and delight in today's pleasure today.

By Tuesday afternoon, the language drills were successfully finished, with Lacy announcing that she had every faith in her pupils' ability to pass their exams. The group then decided that, in celebration, they'd have a bonfire on the beach after supper. Kelly pleaded for a luau, talking mysteriously about cooking things with hot stones buried beneath the sand. The others tossed the suggestion around for a few minutes, until it emerged that no one—including Kelly—had the least idea of how to go about the thing.

"Let's get him!"

"I'd like two ears, matador!"

"Steve! Put that broom down!"

"Can I have Kelly's boots? He won't need them anymore."

"I'm taking 'em with me, pal."

"Boot Hill?"

"He died with his boots on . . ." Steve chanted, strumming the broom handle melodically.

"Bit the dust . . ." Brian chimed in off-key.

"And that's the rust . . ."

". . . of the story!" Lisa and Amy finished soulfully.

Randall winced. "Lord, what a rotten pun."

"The disease is rampant," Lacy told him gravely.

"I thought it was a fever."

"It's progressed to an incurable illness."

"Somebody take that broom away from Steve!" Kelly begged.

Since everyone wanted into the act, supper ended up being a hodgepodge of dishes. Kelly's contribution was judged to be not only inedible but also unidentifiable. Sam, apparently inured to his master's cooking, seemed to enjoy it heartily.

The women cleaned up in the kitchen—it had been the guys the night before—while the men went out to build the bonfire on the beach. Within an hour they were all huddled around the huge fire, bundled in sweaters and jackets and toasting marshmallows.

The group was quiet tonight, perhaps anxious about their upcoming exams. Then again, Lacy thought, an odd instinct seemed to stir to life whenever people gathered in the darkness around a fire. Perhaps it was that. Perhaps they all felt the echoes of a more primitive time. Lacy did.

She was leaning back against Randall, in the hollow of his thighs, with his arms wrapped warmly around her. Staring into the fire silhouetted against darkness, she felt and heard the echoes of a time when darkness was a feared enemy and fire the only weapon against it. When life was today, and only the gods knew what tomorrow would be. When music was an eerie noise made by the wind in the trees, and applause was a clap on the back after a successful hunt.

Lacy listened to the echoes, and something stirred inside her. Some dim, ages-old awareness of life's brief fragility. A growing certainty that today was the day to live for.

How long had human beings lived with fear? Always. Live for today, for tomorrow we may die. But it was true! Everyone lived with the fear of death, but that didn't prevent them from living.

And even though she lived with the fear of loving a celebrity . . . that wouldn't prevent her from loving.

She loved Randall. She had fallen in love with a legend, and then with the man behind it, and that was never going to change. If she walked away from him, she'd be wounded, a part of her torn away. She would always be incomplete, whether she walked away from a friend, a lover, or a husband—because Randall was all those things in her heart.

Randall had music in his soul, and she had Randall in her soul. And if she had to share him with his music tomorrow, she'd cope with that tomorrow. She'd agonize over whether a part of him was better than none of him at all—tomorrow.

The fire came back into focus, smaller now and providing less warmth. Lacy realized in surprise that she and Randall were alone. She turned her head to look back at him. "Where'd everyone go?"

"They drifted away." He smiled. "Two by two."

She laughed a little unsteadily. "I didn't notice."

"You were a million miles away."

A million years, she thought.

"It's getting late, honey—and cold. We'd better go back to the house."

She rose and helped Randall kick sand over the dying fire, feeling the wind cut through her sweater now that she'd left the haven of his arms. And that curiously bereft feeling set the seal on her decision.

They walked back to the house silently, his arm around her shoulders and hers around his waist. The house was dimly lit and quiet, the bedroom doors closed. Except for Lacy's room. And Randall's.

He halted by their doors, looking down at her searchingly. "You're very quiet."

She smiled and shook her head slightly, a gesture

meant to say that nothing was wrong—only a mood that would pass.

He gazed at her steadily for a moment, then half nodded and bent to kiss her lightly. "Good night, honey."

Lacy turned away, slipping into her room and closing the door behind her without responding. She wouldn't say good night to him. Not yet. The lamp on her night-stand left the room in a soft light, enough for her to find what she searched for. Then she headed for the shower.

Half an hour later she stood in front of the full-length mirror in the bathroom and studied her reflection. The nightgown was one that had drawn her eye for lovely things, but she had never worn it until now. Because it was a gown meant to be worn for a man.

It was floor-length shimmering satin, and stark black. Deceptively simple in style and line, it hugged her figure like a loving hand. The skirt fell in a straight line from just beneath her breasts, and the bodice was barely there; it consisted of two small triangles that added little except moral support. Two narrow satin straps tied at the nape of her neck.

She looked good in it. But did she look good enough? Lacy didn't know; she'd never tried to seduce a man before.

Taking a deep breath, she left the bathroom, turning out her lamp on the way through the bedroom. Lights were for people who meant to return, she decided firmly. And she wouldn't be returning tonight.

She hoped.

Randall's door was closed, but Lacy didn't hesitate. Before she could lose her nerve, she opened the door silently, slipped inside, and then closed it. Leaning back against the cool wood, she gazed across the room.

The room was comfortable-looking and furnished with taste, but it contained few symbols of personality. She knew Randall had spent relatively little time here while growing up.

He was lying in the center of the double bed, his hands linked together behind his neck as he gazed pensively at the ceiling. The lamp on his nightstand allowed her to see his expression as he turned his head to look at her, and her anxiety vanished. He wouldn't send her away. Not tonight.

Randall sat up slowly, the covers falling to expose his bare chest. "Lacy..."

"I believe you said something about seduction," she murmured.

He swung his legs over the side of the bed, never taking his eyes off her. She moved slowly toward him, her eyes drinking in the grandeur of his nakedness, until she stood an arm's length away.

"I've had all the time I need, Randall," she told him huskily.

Randall lifted a hand, one finger gently touching the pulse pounding madly in her throat. "So uneasy?" he asked deeply.

"That's not uneasiness." Lacy smiled tremulously. "It's something else."

His hands found her narrow waist, drawing her slowly forward until his lips were at the low neckline of her gown. "Are you sure?" His voice held a hoarse, driven note.

Lacy threaded her fingers through his thick hair. "I'm sure."

Randall rose to his feet, his hands still at her waist and his lips trailing fire up her throat. "Why are you sure?" he pleaded insistently.

"I love you," she whispered, gazing into his eyes and allowing her love for him to show for the first time. "I never stopped loving you."

"Oh, Lacy, I've waited so long to hear you say that!" The hands at her waist pulled her suddenly, almost roughly, against him. "So long...I love you, sweetheart."

She could feel his fierce desire in the hardness of his body and in the strength of the arms sliding around her. And then his mouth was on hers, and her senses spiraled crazily. The primitive hunger bottled up inside her burst free with the power of a fury.

She shivered as his mouth searched, probed. His tongue sought the sensitive inner flesh of her lips, gliding in an intimate caress that sent the strength flowing from her legs. Lacy clung to him desperately, her heart pounding in a rhythm as wild as all unreason. She felt his fingers fumbling with the ties at the nape of her neck and heard his rough laugh as his lips left hers.

"It's almost a crime to take this off," he whispered as the black satin shimmered to the floor. "But it's more than I can stand to leave it on you. You're so beautiful!" His eyes were molten gold as they raked down her naked body with a fixed intensity, and she could feel their searing brand through every pore.

Nothing separated them now; flesh met flesh in a surge of inescapable need, and both of them gasped at the instant, soul-jarring shock. Randall possessed her lips again, his hands dropping to her hips and pulling her even closer, until not even a sigh could have slipped between them. Lacy felt her nipples swelling and hardening, the mat of black hair on his chest teasing sensuously.

A moment later she felt herself being lifted, and then softness cushioned her as Randall's body bore her down into his bed. His mouth sought her breasts, moving from one to the other with yearning hunger. Lacy kept her fingers locked in his hair, holding him to her with a hunger of her own.

She could feel the tension building within her, storming through her body in a steadily increasing force until it erupted with a savagery she would not have believed possible, and she became the wildcat he had once compared her to. No longer afraid of the elemental passion he could unleash, Lacy took fire in his arms.

Only dimly aware of the throaty growl emerging from deep in her throat—or deep in her soul—Lacy searched out the rippling muscles of his back and shoulders, exploring in an attempt to satisfy her hunger. Her nails scratched lightly, the pads of her fingers soothing each tiny wound. She was aware of his hands molding, shaping her willing flesh, of his mouth's hot demand, and her body moved with a restless impatience she didn't even try to control.

She abandoned herself to sensation, arching against him with a craving to be a part of him, with a need that went far beyond reason.

"Lacy!" His features were taut, his voice a harsh rasp in his throat. A golden blaze flared in his honey eyes as he settled himself between her thighs.

Lacy could sense the slender thread of his control, and she wanted to snap that thread. An instinct deeper than her soul, older than Eve, compelled her to rouse the beast, the basic, primitive male held captive all these years by a legend—and by a civilized man. It became imperative to release him as she had been released.

Instead of being the possessed, Lacy became the possessor. Fiercely, she caught him within herself, forging a bond as strong as tempered steel, as fine as a silken thread. Her movements held the grace of ballet and the turbulent power of nature rebelling. She marked him with her own brand of loving.

And the basic male within Randall surfaced with crucial, flaming need. His own strength and power stopped just this side of savagery, enveloping her in a detonation of raw passion.

It was a violent, tempestuous joining. In the eye of a scalding storm, they clung together, feeding the fire until it burst forth in a blinding incandescence, cauterizing old wounds and sealing forever the bond between them. And then the flame died slowly, settling softly into embers awaiting only a willing breath to set them ablaze once again...

The lamplit room was quiet and still, the sounds of harsh breathing growing softer as hearts gradually returned to normal. They rested in each other's arms, as if neither could bear to be even a whisper away from the other.

Lacy was limp, utterly sated, and curiously at peace. She didn't want to move. Let the world go on without her. Let time twist and turn or stop altogether. She didn't care.

And then the silence of the room yielded to a soft, awed voice.

"Lord," Randall murmured huskily, "I've dreamed

that a hundred times—asleep and awake. But the dreams pale beside reality." He raised up on an elbow, looking down at her with gold's warm glow in his eyes. "It was beautiful, love."

She linked her fingers together behind his neck, smiling up at him contentedly. "Worth all these days?" she teased softly.

Randall's smile twisted a little. "Worth all these days. Laughter aside, I was about to go crazy." His hand brushed a strand of raven hair off her forehead and then stroked her cheek gently. "I love you, Lacy."

"I love you," she whispered unsteadily.

He kissed her tenderly, adoringly. "My darling. My Lacy." In a sudden change of tone he added calmly, "And if you leave me again, when I catch you, I'll turn you over my knee."

Lacy blinked. "Macho."

"To the core."

She swallowed a giggle. "I see. Is that a warning?"

"I thought it was only fair."

"So you'll resort to caveman tactics if I, um, get out of line?"

Randall reached to pull the covers up around them snugly. "Yes. And don't blame me for it. You let him out."

"I what?" This time the giggle escaped.

"You let him out. The caveman." Randall wore a perfectly solemn face. "A few minutes ago. You unlocked his cage and let him out. Didn't you hear him beating on his chest? I heard him."

Lacy laughed outright. "I let him out, huh? Does that mean he's mine?"

Randall considered. "I think *he* thinks you're his."

"Ah."

"Do you mind?" Randall asked anxiously. "I can't seem to do anything with him; he's out of control."

"I see."

"Maybe we could tame him?"

Lacy smiled slowly. "Let's not do that."

"You like him wild?"

"He has certain...admirable qualities," she murmured.

"For instance?" Randall asked politely.

"Don't make me blush."

"Oh."

"Indeed."

"You're knocking all feminist ideals into a cocked hat, you know."

"Ah, well. Can't fight a cavewoman."

"Cave*woman?*"

"Uh-huh. *You* let *her* out."

"I did?"

"In spades."

"How about that? I thought it was my imagination."

"What was?"

"That wildcat's growl I heard."

"It *was* your imagination."

"No. You're blushing, by the way."

"You're imagining again."

"Sorry."

Lacy frowned at him, well aware of the grin he was trying hard to hide. "Tell your caveman to stop beating on his chest."

"Do I have to?"

"Yes. Enough's enough."

Hands began wandering beneath the covers.

"You were saying?" Randall murmured, trailing feath-erlight kisses down her throat.

Lacy gasped softly. "I—was saying that enough was enough." She gasped again. "But I didn't say—that I'd had enough..."

A willing breath set the embers ablaze.

When Randall reached to turn out the lamp some time later, Lacy roused herself enough to murmur sleepily, "Somebody give that caveman a box of cigars."

Randall chuckled in the darkness and held her close.

Lacy awoke to the warmth of a lover—and had ab-solutely no fault to find with the arrangement. She was lying on her back, close beside Randall. His arm lay heavily across her middle, and his face was nuzzled into the curve of her neck. She could feel his steady, warm breath on her skin, and a peaceful contentment stole over her.

Experimentally, she moved, smiling when his arm tightened around her even in sleep. Completely unwilling to leave him, she lay in comfort and watched a brilliant ray of sunshine cast its narrow spotlight between the opening of the curtains. She struggled for a moment to remember which side of the house that window was on. East. Morning sun, then.

It must be around eight, she decided. She listened to the silence of the house for a moment. Odd that the kids weren't up. Every one of them seemed to be an early bird. A dim awareness tugged at her mind, seeking at-tention. Something about a door. Her bedroom door? Had she closed it last night? No...

Doors.

Lacy shifted her head to one side slightly so as not to disturb Randall, then lifted it, directing her gaze toward the door. Naturally, it was unlocked. Wouldn't it be hell if—

There was a sudden thud against the door; a charitable soul might have called it a knock.

Randall's head lifted from the pillow as if he'd been shot. And, like Lacy, once his eyes were open, he was entirely awake. He blinked once, and a warm golden glow kindled to life in his eyes as he looked at her.

"Good morning, love," he murmured, kissing her before she could respond.

"Um . . . Randall," she managed when the kiss began to trail down her neck. "I think we're about to have—"

The door crashed open.

"—company," she finished dryly, checking hastily to make sure the covers were doing what they were supposed to do—covering.

It was Kelly, of course. Lynn and her friends were leaving today, and Lacy decided with amusement that it was entirely appropriate that Kelly's parting gift to them would be another interruption.

As unembarrassed as she was, Randall half turned to glare toward the open door. "Professor . . ." he began sternly.

"Well, well." Unabashed, Kelly crossed his arms over his chest and leaned against the jamb, merry blue eyes filled with laughter. "Fancy this. And I thought you two'd have to be stranded in the Arctic with a single sleeping bag before you'd, um, cohabitate."

"You thought?" Randall's glare deepened. "You've done everything in your power to keep us apart, you—you bearded fruitcake!"

"Who, me?" Kelly looked innocence itself. "I just thought you'd welcome a bit of...um...spice in the chase."

Randall turned and sat up, careful not to compromise Lacy's modesty by dislodging the covers. "Professor, I'm going to get you for this," he said courteously.

"You'll have to catch me first, piano player." Kelly's grin widened. "And we both know who can outrun who."

"That's *whom*," another voice corrected, and Lynn leaned casually against the jamb opposite Kelly. Her golden eyes were bright. "Hello, you two," she greeted cheerfully. "I'm glad to see you finally got around to it."

"I was planning to get them one for Christmas," Kelly confided to her seriously.

"One what?"

"A round tuit, of course."

Lynn dropped her chin in a gesture of despair. "Oh, Lord."

"Would it do me any good to tell you two to leave?" Randall asked wryly.

"No." Kelly looked soulful. "Love in bloom; I just get a kick out of watching."

"There's a word for that," Randall told him.

"Yeah?"

"Yeah. Voyeurism."

"Such language. And in front of the ladies."

Steve appeared suddenly in the doorway. "Hello."

"Hello," Randall replied politely.

"Nice day," Steve offered, straight-faced.

"It started out that way."

Brian peered around Steve. *"E pluribus unum,"* he offered solemnly.

That was when Lacy came apart.

Randall cleared his throat determinedly.

"They're not many," Kelly pointed out critically.

"No, but they're—"

"Out!" Randall ordered.

Brian looked hurt, and vanished. None of the others made a move to leave, and Brian's absence was immediately filled by Amy and Lisa.

"Good morning!" they chorused, and Lisa added spritely, "Shall we serve you breakfast in bed?"

"I'm going to count to three," Randall began.

"And then?" Kelly asked interestedly.

"Murder," Randall promised with a wolfish grin.

"For breakfast?" Lynn asked.

"For you—all of you."

"Just what I always wanted," Steve murmured.

Randall dropped his head into his hands.

"I wanted a train set," Kelly announced mournfully.

"Set where?" Steve asked curiously.

"I wanted a tea set," Amy said.

"Set where?"

"A television set," Lisa tossed in.

"Set *where?*"

"The air's getting thick with bad puns," Randall groaned. "Somebody open a window. Or better yet, close a door. Behind you. On your way out."

"I feel a hint in the air," Kelly said. "We'd better clear out, guys. Randy's looking dangerous."

"I told you not to call me that."

"I'd say that was the least of your complaints right now."

"True. Are you leaving, or not?"

Kelly had cheerfully shoved the others out into the

hall, and he now stood holding the doorknob.

"Ask me nicely."

"I'll ask you with a loaded gun."

"Why is Lacy's head under the covers?" Kelly asked suddenly.

Lacy, who had been giggling almost nonstop since the unannounced entry into their bedroom, peered over the covers with laughing eyes. "If Randall doesn't kill you, I will!" she promised unsteadily.

"In that case, I'll be leaving," Kelly told them disdainfully. "I know when I'm not wanted."

"Good-bye," Randall said.

The door closed behind Kelly with gentle dignity.

When Randall fell back onto the pillow beside her, Lacy was laughing almost too hard to speak. Even as she felt the despairing chuckles shaking him, she managed to control her amusement enough to get a few words out.

"In the public eye—with your clothes off!"

"I'll kill him," Randall groaned. "I will definitely kill that bearded fruitcake!"

CHAPTER
Nine

BY NOON THE kids had gone, their leave-taking as bois-
terous as everything else had been. Frantic questions
about who had packed what in whose car were shouted
back and forth right up until the time the cars pulled out
of the driveway.

Randall hugged Lynn, which seemed to surprise both
of them, and then rather hastily told her to plan on spending at least a couple of weeks at the cabin during the
coming summer. Their family needed unity, he told her,
and he meant to see that they began building that unity.

He and Lacy stood outside, watching the cars pull
away and returning cheerful waves. As the last car disappeared, Lacy glanced up to see a somewhat bemused
expression on Randall's face.

"What did Kelly say to you a minute ago?" she asked

curiously. "He had a conspiratorial air about him."

"He said," Randall murmured, "that he'd be my best man if I'd be his."

Lacy laughed. "Sounds like him! Are you going to take him up on it?" It didn't hit her until then just what she was asking.

"That depends," He looked down at her soberly. "I'd like to, but he said it'd be an even trade. My participation in his wedding—for his participation in mine."

"It's cold out here," she said brightly, and she quickly retreated into the house.

Randall was right on her heels.

"Lacy . . ."

"What do you think about lunch? I knew we had a late breakfast, but—"

"Lacy, you can't avoid the subject. I won't let you."

She went into the den, finding herself gazing at the piano in the corner as though it were the stuff of nightmares. And for her, it was. She turned away from its gleaming mockery, standing by the hearth and gazing down at the ashes of yesterday's fire.

Randall followed her into the room.

"Has Kelly told Lynn of his intentions?" she wondered aloud, still trying to avoid that other topic. "Knowing him, he probably hasn't. Has it ever occurred to him that she'll turn him down?"

"Do you think she will?"

Her peripheral vision and every sense in her body told Lacy that Randall was standing just behind her right shoulder, looking at her steadily. She shook her head slowly in answer to his question. "No. No, I don't think she will."

"Neither do I."

She tried for a light note. "So you'll have a bearded fruitcake for a brother-in-law."

"Looks that way."

Desperately, she made another attempt. "You'll have to brush up on your puns. And you'll have to—"

"Lacy!"

She was turned swiftly, his hands forcing her around to face him. And his expression was a determined one.

"Stop it, Lacy. Stop it and tell me what's wrong," he insisted quietly.

Lacy looked up to see the anxiety mixed with determination in his face, and she realized that she had to make him understand. "Randall, I don't want to think about tomorrow—not now. It's something I began to understand only last night. *Today* is so important. You and I spent a lot of time fighting our way through yesterday. We've only now been able to leave it behind us, where it belongs."

She reached up to touch his lean cheek, hoping that what she saw in his golden eyes was understanding. "We have today. And I want us to *live* in today for a while. I want us to live as though yesterday didn't exist and tomorrow might not happen."

His hands framed her face warmly. "And when tomorrow comes?" he asked softly.

Lacy smiled slightly. "Then it comes. And we'll be ready for it." She hesitated for a moment. "Randall, the man I've gotten to know these last few days has surprised me. His warmth and his humor. His willingness—even determination—to be a brother for the first time in his life.

"I'm still learning what he's all about, still discovering him." Her lips curved in a sudden smile. "Like that caveman who came out of hiding last night; that was a part of him. And like the part of him who was wonderfully good-natured and humorous over an...untimely interruption this morning."

She searched for the right words, and Randall supplied them quietly.

"You still need time."

Lacy gazed at him anxiously. "Do you understand? Last night was a step—a big one. But there are other steps, and they have to be taken one at a time. I love you, Randall. I want to be your friend and your lover."

"And my wife?" he asked huskily.

Her heart lurched, then steadied. "If that's where the steps lead us." She smiled. "You're learning to enjoy life, Randall, to play at it. So, let's play for a while. Let's laugh and love and be together."

He looked down at her for a long moment, and then nodded slowly. "One step at a time, then. But fair warning." His smile was crooked. "Those steps lead to the altar. And that's where we'll be eventually. Even if I have to throw you over my shoulder for those last few steps."

Lacy cocked her head to one side as though listening to a distant sound. "Did I just hear a certain caveman beating on his chest?"

"I believe you did."

"Hmmm. Why do I get the feeling that he has a few irritating as well as admirable qualities?"

"I can't imagine." Randall smiled slowly, his hands dropping to span her waist and draw her closer. "But just remember, love—you let him out."

* * *

In the days that followed, Lacy had cause to delight in that admirable and irritating caveman's release.

The weather warmed and began to resemble the spring it was supposed to be, giving them the whole outdoors to play in. And play they did. Not a word was spoken between them of futures, even as far as tomorrow. From the time they woke up in each other's arms until the time they fell asleep in each other's arms, every moment was filled with spontaneity.

And the qualities that had only just began to emerge in Randall during the first few days now blossomed. He was warm and funny and sometimes absurd. He couldn't let even a few minutes go by without touching Lacy, even if the touch were only a finger touching her nose or a pat on the fanny. And the caveman's release made him wonderfully unpredictable.

"Randall?"

"Yes, sweetheart?"

"I'm not a sack of grain."

"I'm so glad."

"So why am I hanging over your shoulder like a sack of grain?"

"I want to show you something."

"I can't see whatever it is on my own two feet?"

"This is faster."

"Tell the caveman to stop beating his chest."

"It's too late. He's run amok."

"Well, where is he taking me?"

"To a cove."

"Why?"

"Ravishment."

"Oh. How nice. I haven't been ravished in days."

"Liar. You were ravished yesterday."

"I was?"

"You mean you don't remember?"

"I remember that fruit punch you concocted."

"The ravishment came after."

"Ah. Is that why I woke up this morning with a flower in my hair?"

"Uh-huh."

"It seemed odd at the time."

"I'm sure."

"Randall?"

"Hmmm?"

"There's a couple down the beach waving at us."

"Well, wave back."

"I think they think I'm being abducted."

"Then give 'em thumbs-up."

"Right."

"What did they do?"

"They're going the other way now."

"Good. Ravishment demands privacy."

"Randall?"

"Yes, love?"

"The blood's rushing to my head."

"The better to make you dizzy with passion."

Their afternoon at the cove was one of many "adventures" for the two of them. Not all were passionate; some were comical. And all of them delighted Lacy.

"Randall, that's not possible."

"Sure it is."

"It's not. You just can't *do* that!"

"Why?"

"Because."

"Try again."

"No. I don't have your balance."

"You have grace. Far more important."

"Bathtubs weren't designed for this."

"I can't stand rejection."

"I'm not rejecting you."

"I'm hurt, Lacy. I'm horribly hurt."

"Oh!"

"Hmmm. Now aren't you glad you tried again?"

"Was this the caveman's idea?"

"Certainly."

"Give that man a cigar..."

The "caveman" had released a part of Randall, and Lacy loved that. But something else had been released within him as well, and she forgave Kelly his untimely interruptions, his terrible puns, and everything else. She forgave him and planned to kiss him if she ever saw him again, because he had helped to free humor and rebellion in Randall.

His humor was a constant thing now, and Lacy wholeheartedly encouraged it. No matter how absurd or ridiculous his mood, she egged him on, because it was such a wonderful contrast to the disciplined man who had lived and breathed only serious music.

His rebellion reared its head somewhat unexpectedly one morning, and tickled Lacy's sense of humor as nothing else had.

Waking up to find her caveman in a playful mood, Lacy was preparing to engage him in a passionate game— winner take all—when she suddenly became aware of a subtle change in his kisses. What was different about them? And then she realized.

"Um, Randall?"

Warm, drugging lips were moving down her throat. "You're fined three kisses for talking out of turn," he murmured.

She locked her fingers in his hair and firmly pulled his head up. "Randall, are you—You are! You're growing a mustache!"

"Oh, you noticed, did you?"

"I knew there was something different."

He looked suddenly sheepish. "You don't mind, do you?"

"Mind? Why should I mind?" Her head tilted to one side critically. "In fact, it adds a certain something."

"It adds an itch," he complained wryly.

Lacy started to giggle. "So tell me. Why this unexpected urge to decorate your face?"

"Well . . . I've never rebelled in my life. Thought I'd give it a try."

"Kelly got to you," she translated affably.

"Nonsense."

"He got to you. He stroked his macho beard, and he got to you. Admit it!"

"If that's what you think, I'll shave it off."

"Don't you dare!" Lacy kissed him, her manner one of dispassionate experimentation. "I like it much better."

"Better than what?"

"Better than before."

"You didn't like it before?" he asked, wounded.

"It needed spice," she confided solemnly.

"Gee, thanks."

"Don't mention it."

"I'd like to."

"Like to what?"

"Mention it."

"Oh, have I trodden on your ego?"

"Well, don't mind that. I mean, what's an ego for if not to be trampled on?"

"I said 'tread' not 'trample.'"

"If a difference doesn't *make* a difference, then it isn't a difference."

Lacy ran the statement through her mind. "I can't decipher that at eight o'clock in the morning," she told him finally.

"I just said that tread or trample doesn't make a difference. They're both the same. Painful."

"Poor baby."

"You're a cruel woman, Lacy Hamilton."

"One has to be in order to cope with a caveman."

"Speaking of which..."

"Oh, is he getting impatient?"

"Can't you hear him beating on his chest?"

"We need to teach him an alternate method of expressing himself."

"Why?"

"He must be black and blue by now."

"Are you kidding? Cavemen are tough."

"Macho."

"They invented it."

"I see."

"Um, Lacy, what're you doing?"

"Well, what do you think?"

"I think, my love, that the caveman has met his match."

"'Oh, what a falling off was there,'" she murmured.

"And no net to catch the poor guy."

"That rotten pun will cost *you* three kisses..."

* * *

Within a couple of days Randall's mustache had come forth in all its glory, and the change it wrought in his face was amazing. Given his classically handsome features, Lacy decided, the bit of rebellion was almost necessary; classical tended to be cold, and the mustache added a bold and jaunty dash of liveliness.

Lacy trimmed it for him, threatening laughingly to hide his razor until a beard grew. But she didn't; she agreed with Randall's assertion that he didn't need *that* much rebellion on his face. Besides, she decided inwardly, hiding that much of his face would be a crime against nature.

As the days slipped past, they grew closer to one another. In love and in humor. They talked and laughed and made love. And learned each other.

It was their first opportunity to really spend time alone, just the two of them. And that time was spent as though each moment were precious. No knocks on the door, no ringing telephones, no demands.

No interruptions.

It proved to Lacy that more than passion held them together. They made love, certainly. But they also made happiness for each other.

And they made music.

Lacy was reponsible for that. She was worried because Randall hadn't touched the piano since they'd arrived: he hadn't so much as looked at it.

A part of her wanted the legend to be a thing of the past. But she was afraid of what that might do to Randall. And if this time of discovery had healed whatever had gone wrong with Randall's music, then the star, she knew, would rise from the ashes of his defeat and glitter more brightly than ever.

The music world would reclaim its legend.

And that was what she feared, the dread hanging over her like the sword of Damocles. She could share Randall with his music; she knew that. But she couldn't share him with the demands of his celebrity. Those demands would tear her apart, tear them apart. Concert tours, endless practicing, endless rehearsing, parties, benefits, society functions. No time for a life together, no time for a home and children. No time.

And even realizing that, Lacy had to do what she could to rebuild the legend. Randall had asked her once to help him find out what was wrong. In vulnerability and weariness and pain, he'd asked her to help him.

So she put off tomorrow, turning her gaze away from the vision of an empty future.

And she tried to help him.

A chilly evening sent Randall out to get wood for a fire, and when he returned with an armful, Lacy was seated at the piano playing a light, popular tune. She'd decided not to attempt a classical piece; although her memory was excellent, her fingers were out of practice.

From the corner of her eye she saw Randall pause in the doorway and watch her for a few moments, then come into the room and silently build the fire. Only when it was blazing brightly did he approach the piano.

"Not bad," he noted critically, sitting down on the bench beside her.

Grinning at him, Lacy swung suddenly into a jaunty jazz piece, playing entirely from memory and not doing badly at all.

"A little help from the maestro, please!"

Laughing, Randall joined in, his long fingers moving

over the keys with the ease of thirty years' hard work. If he realized himself that it was the first time he'd played since the botched concert, it wasn't apparent.

And Lacy had counted on that. She'd chosen music far different from the classical, and by treating the whole thing lightly she hoped to ease him back into playing with no demand, no insistence on the precise, the mathmatically exact.

And her instincts were right.

That first step led to another and another. She teased him playfully about the music he'd mentioned composing, launched spirited arguments over which old master had been the best, and asked for his criticism on her own playing.

A day passed, and then another. Light discussions became serious ones, and the classics replaced jazz and pop. Bits of works were picked out to illustrate one point or another. Sheet music was found and studied. Randall even gave in to her pleas and played one of his own compositions for her, and she wasn't at all surprised to find that it was more than good.

Relaxed and at ease before the keyboard, Randall seemed more sensitive to the music than he had ever been before. He *listened* to it and, more important, he heard it. The music came from inside him, and it wasn't blocked or distorted now by obsession or by a star's reflective glitter. He made music for the sheer pleasure of hearing it, and the music he made was incredibly good.

Brilliant.

Lacy had forgotten just how good he was. She listened, enthralled, held spellbound by the genius of his touch. The magic. He painted a mood with sound, gave it texture and substance, and made it come alive. It soared and glided, a winged miracle to enchant.

Never had she understood so well what the music meant to him. He was telling her with each seemingly effortless stroke of a key, with each note. And never had she appreciated his gift so much. She knew now why he had sacrificed for it, knew what the music had demanded of him. He could never have been less than a legend, she realized.

And though the legend may have been crumbling, a strange and magical catharsis seemed to have taken place. The man had thrown off his obsession and pushed aside the legend, and he had walked through the fire to find out what was beneath the glitter, emerging with a stronger sense of himself.

The glitter, she realized, was gone. The legend had become the man. He was whole, complete. The world could heap on him glitter of its own, and the world would be blinded by it just as before. But no one who knew him would ever again be blinded by the fool's gold.

Because the real thing shone from him and soared in his music.

Lacy listened to the magic, and she couldn't blame the world for heaping glitter on him. She felt sorry for them because they couldn't see the true gold. But she envied them, too.

Because she was very much afraid that, though the world would never have all of him again, it would have a great deal of his time. Perhaps all of his time.

And she didn't know where that left her.

CHAPTER
Ten

LACY WASN'T GOING to run away again. She knew that.
But she also knew that loving a legend meant sharing
him with the world. It meant knowing that their life would
be, in a sense, public property. It meant no time for a
normal home life; it meant living out of suitcases while
touring, or waiting at home for him to come back.

Waiting. Waiting while the demands of a world were
dealt with first.

Taking second place.

She couldn't do that. In the end it would tear her
apart. Tear them both apart. But how could she tell him
that?

Randall's composition died into silence, and Lacy,
watching from one corner of the loveseat, was silently
grateful that the only light in the room came from the

lamp over the piano. She needed time to compose herself.

It was Friday night; the two weeks Randall had suggested were nearly over. She was due back at work on Monday.

And tomorrow was here.

"That was beautiful," she said huskily as he left the piano and moved across the room to her.

"I'm glad you like it." Randall automatically turned on the lamp just behind the loveseat before joining her.

"I loved it." Lacy dropped her lashes to hide eyes that were hot with suppressed tears. She welcomed the familiar warmth of his arm as it slid around her, and she wondered again how to tell him, how to make him understand.

"Lacy? Why are you hiding those beautiful jade eyes from me?" He was smiling as he tipped her chin up, but the smile immediately vanished as he read the misery in her expression. Concerned golden eyes searched her face.

And with the closeness now between them, he knew what was wrong. "Tomorrow," he said quietly.

Almost inaudibly, her own voice choked off somewhere near her soul, she said, "You have your music back now, Randall. You don't need me anymore."

"I'll always need you," he insisted softly. "Lacy, I love you. I want to spend the rest of my life with you!"

"Your world is too demanding," she said. "Randall, I'll never willingly leave you again. But there are just too many demands on you, on your time, and on us. I want a family, a settled home. I've lived out of a suitcase for too many years."

"I want a home, too," he told her quietly. "A home with you, a home with our children."

"What about your music? What about your . . . world?"

"You've freed me of that world, Lacy." His voice was clear and certain. "You freed me by showing me what life is like outside of it. I understand now what I never did before: that I *have* lived in a different kind of world. A confining world. I never realized all the things missing from that world until you came into my life and began to show me. But you did show me. You helped me push the legend aside and leave it behind me. And I don't *want* that legend back, Lacy!"

"But . . . that first day . . . you were worried about something being wrong, about something being different. And you made mistakes."

"I was a nervous wreck." He smiled faintly. "You never realized what you did to me. I don't think you realize even now. I could barely concentrate on stringing words together to make intelligible sentences. That explains the mistakes. And I was worried about the music, Lacy. I thought it was changing. But it was never really the music; it was me. And I was changing because of you."

"Because of me?"

"You walked into my world, and I began to see it through your eyes. I didn't realize it then. I didn't understand what was happening to me. But I knew you were responsible. I saw things in a new light. Little things at first—the absurdity of bodyguards, for instance."

Lacy couldn't help but smile.

Randall touched her cheek gently. "When you flung everything into my face and left, I sat down and did some hard thinking. What baffled me the most was your contention that the demands of my career—the interruptions—were too much to take." He sighed. "I'm ashamed to say that I barely noticed the interruptions, I suppose because I was so accustomed to them.

"But then"—he smiled crookedly—"I spent some time in *your* world. A real world filled with real people. Normal day-to-day activities. Wondering who'd take out the garbage or cook dinner or wash dishes. No special consideration for a—a star out of his element. And I realized just how annoying interruptions could be."

Lacy silently resolved to kiss Kelly *twice*.

"And it wasn't only the interruptions. I began to see very clearly what I'd been missing. A home life. Time to spend with other people, talking about something other than music. Relationships with people that were unclouded by who and what I am—uninfluenced by fame.

"Being treated as a normal man—nothing else—for the first time in my life. I didn't know I'd missed that, Lacy. But I know now."

After a moment, she said slowly, "The concert ... You were upset about us, weren't you? That's why your concentration went."

He nodded. "Shook me up a little," he murmured. "That's never happened to me before. Not on stage. I've never lost my concentration so completely. And it happened then because, for the first time in my life, something mattered more than the music. It mattered so much that I couldn't shut it out. Mattered so much that thirty years of training couldn't stand against it." Softly, roughly, he told her, "You're the only person in the world who's ever mattered more to me than my music. The only person in the world who can make me act against my own nature."

Randall held her hand firmly. "Lacy, my music is the way it was once, long ago, when it was new. When I played for the sheer joy of hearing the music and didn't give a damn about being the best. I feel the music for the first time in years."

He looked at her steadily, and she tried to blink away her tears. He continued decisively, "And it's because you've shown me how to open up. You've given me that. You've taught me to look at the music from the right perspective and to give it its proper place in my life. You taught me that by bringing me into the real world and showing me what was important—really important—to me."

Squeezing her hand to keep her from interrupting, he went on, "Without you, half of me is gone—locked away somewhere in that other world. And I don't just mean my music. These last weeks . . . I've learned to enjoy life, Lacy. I don't want to lose that. I can't lose you."

She swallowed the lump in her throat. "I heard the difference in your music tonight. The critics—the world—will be ecstatic when they hear it. And the star will glow brighter than ever. The demands on you, on your time, will be heavier than they've ever been before."

He stirred slightly and started to speak, but she placed trembling fingers across his lips.

"Concert tours and publicity and the spotlight—I can't take that, Randall! I can share you with your music, but I can't share you with the world! I knew that; I knew it all along. But I wouldn't let myself think about it because it hurt so much.

"When I thought you'd lost your music, when I thought the legend was crumbling," she rushed on painfully, "for one awful moment, I was *glad!*" A sob escaped her. "Because there's nothing more quickly forgotten than old news and yesterday's legend, and I knew I wouldn't have to share you with them anymore! I was glad, Randall, and I hated myself for that!"

"Darling..." He turned her face up with gentle urgency, his voice hoarse when he went on. "Sweetheart, did you ever think that I might be tired of the spotlight? That I might be all too willing to be yesterday's legend? Don't you realize that that's what I've been telling you?"

She tried to see his face through tear-blurred eyes, his words sinking in slowly. "But... all these years—"

"Yes," he interrupted with soft fierceness. "All these years. Nearly thirty years. Practicing day in and day out, burying myself in my work until I didn't even know if I was *real* anymore! My family are strangers to me, and it took you and a—a bearded fruitcake to teach me how to laugh again!"

A tearful giggle escaped Lacy, and there was a bright gleam of response in Randall's eyes. Then he was going on quietly, "Thirty years, and what did it get me? Ability? I'm no better technically now than I was ten years ago. Money? Sure, but I had enough then, too. Fame? It wasn't what I wanted. I wanted to be the best. Well, they called me the best ten years ago; I should have had the sense to quit then."

"Why didn't you."

"You were right, Lacy. I've been obsessed for a long time. I let the music control me. But I'm in control now, and I plan to become yesterday's legend just as fast as I can!"

Lacy swallowed hard, afraid to believe in this. "Are you sure you won't regret it?" she asked in a whisper.

Randall shook his head. "Honey, I made up my mind

to quit when you walked across that stage. I saw what I'd lost, what I was afraid I'd lost forever, and the concert halls weren't that important anymore."

"What will you do?" She knew that Randall wasn't the type of man who could sit and do nothing.

"First, I'd like to learn how to be a brother and a son." He smiled at her slowly, tenderly. "And a husband and father."

"And later?"

"I want to compose. Give concerts only occasionally—and only near home. And I've been asked to teach at several of the universities. I think I'd like that. I've recently developed grave fears for today's youth!" He grinned, then sobered again. "It doesn't really matter, Lacy. I'll always have the music; all the rest is just garbage." He looked at her with sudden anxiety in his eyes. "I love you, darling. I want you to go on teaching me to play at life—for the rest of our lives. Marry me?"

Lacy felt herself drowning in the honey sweetness of his eyes, and a burden lifted from her heart. "Tomorrow we can call Lynn and Kelly," she said softly, "and tell them they've just been elected maid of honor and best man, respectively."

In a single movement Randall was off the loveseat and lifting her up into his arms, swinging her around in a dizzying whirl and then striding toward the bedroom with her in his arms.

"Oh, sweetheart, I thought we'd never make it!" He kissed her almost fiercely, his mustache a sensuous caress.

Lacy clung to him happily.

* * *

A long time later, they lay in each other's arms and talked softly, both reluctant to disturb the midnight quiet of the lamplit room.

"Andrew will have kittens when I quit," Lacy murmured.

Randall drew her even closer. "Don't forget you have one more assignment as translator for the last Randall St. James European concert tour," he teased. More seriously he continued, "I hope you won't regret giving up your job, sweetheart."

"Of course I won't. I'll be too busy. I have to learn how to be a wife and mother, you know. And, later, I might decide to do some teaching myself. I enjoyed working with Lynn and her friends."

"Are you sure? About giving up your job, I mean."

"Look, laddie, if y'think I'm goin' to dash off to Europe at Andrew Preston's whim and leave you alone to fight off the women anxious for y'favors, you've got another think comin'!"

"That was a very good Scottish accent."

"It ought to be; I'm Scottish on both sides."

"Highland temper?"

"It's dreadful."

"I'll bear that in mind.

"You're not punning again, are you?"

"Bite your tongue."

"Sorry."

"Shall we visit bonnie Scotland on our honeymoon, or have you seen the ancestral soil once too often?"

"Oddly enough, I've never set foot there."

"Shall we, then?"

"As long as it's *after* this last tour—not *during* it—anywhere with you, darling."

"You know," he said softly, "that's the first time you've called me that."

"If you don't like it..." she began teasingly.

"Oh, I like it. In fact, I'd love to hear it as often as possible."

"Then consider it my gift to you, darling."

"I'll always treasure it." He raised up on an elbow and kissed her tenderly, remaining there to gaze down at her.

Smiling, Lacy brought the hand she was holding up to her lips in a gesture almost of worship. Worship for a man—not a god. Worship for a lover—not a legend.

Randall's eyes darkened, and she felt a slight tremor in his hand. His gaze shifted to their entwined fingers for a moment, then back to her face. "If I were in an accident tomorrow and lost my hands," he said in a deep, driven voice, "it wouldn't tear me apart to never be able to feel a piano's keys beneath my fingers." He lifted her hand to his lips. "It would tear me apart to never again be able to reach out and touch you."

Lacy felt her heart stop and then begin to beat in a slow, awed rhythm. Her free hand lifted to curve around his neck, pulling him down until she could kiss him with all the love aching inside herself.

"I love you," she whispered against his lips.

"And I love you." He smiled down at her, honey eyes lightened by golden sparks of mischief. "The caveman's shouting 'Mine!'" he murmured.

"That's all right." Her smile was demure. "The cavewoman doesn't mind a bit."

CHAPTER
Eleven

RANDALL WAS FIRST out the door, holding it for Lacy and balancing his burden on one hip. "Sure you can manage that?" he asked in concern. "We can switch if you'd like."

"No, I'm fine the way—" Lacy began. She was interrupted by a strange voice.

"Excuse me, but aren't you—" The smartly dressed, middle-aged woman broke off in mid-query as she clearly took a better look at Randall.

She saw a tall man in jeans and a casual shirt, his classical facial features half hidden by a luxuriant mustache. He wore a wide gold wedding band and sported a black-haired, green-eyed baby on his hip.

Lacy nearly burst out laughing as she watched the

179

woman's face assume distant politeness and heard stiffness coat her voice.

"Pardon me; you reminded me of someone." Taking
advantage of the still-open door, she swept inside.

Randall allowed the door to swing shut behind the
woman as he was momentarily distracted. Eight-month-
old Adam tugged gleefully on his father's mustache.
Wincing, Randall patiently removed the chubby fingers.
"Mind your manners, young man!" he warned with a
mock scowl, which appeared to delight Adam no end.

Lacy shifted two shopping bags and a diaper bag to
her left arm, then slipped her free arm through Randall's.
"Another ex-fan, darling?" she asked with a nod in the
direction the woman had disappeared in.

Randall's gaze followed hers for a moment, then he
shrugged philosophically. "Ah, well," he said cheerfully,
"they all have to learn."

"Learn what?" Lacy asked.

"That old legends never die. They just get married
and learn to change diapers."

Lacy was still laughing as they started down the bus-
tling New York sidewalk.

All of the above titles are $1.95
Prices may be slightly higher in Canada.

HERE'S WHAT READERS ARE SAYING ABOUT

Second Chance at Love ®

"I think your books are great. I love to read them as does my family."
— P. S., Milford. MA*

"Your books are some of the best romances I've read."
— M. B., Zeeland. MI*

"SECOND CHANCE AT LOVE is my favorite line of romance novels."
— L. B., Springfield. VA*

"I think SECOND CHANCE AT LOVE books are terrific. I married my 'Second Chance' over 15 years ago. I truly believe love is lovelier the second time around!"
— P. P., Houston. TX*

"I enjoy your books tremendously."
— I. S., Bayonne. NJ*

"I love your books and read them all the time. Keep them coming—they're just great."
— G. L., Brookfield. CT*

"SECOND CHANCE AT LOVE books are definitely the best!"
— D. P., Wabash, IN*

*Name and address available upon request